I0784631

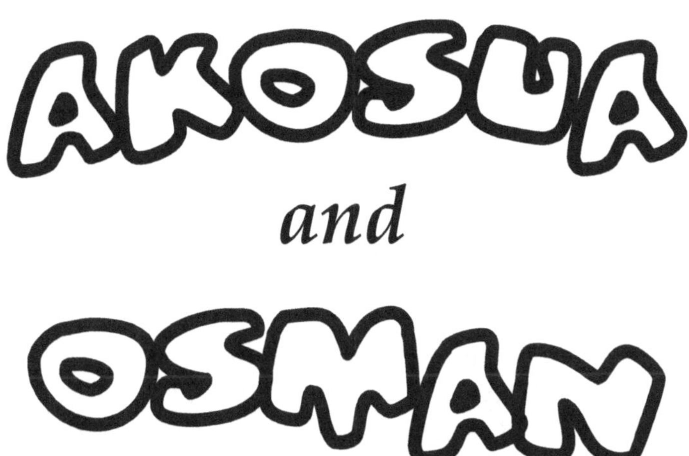

AKOSUA

and

OSMAN

Also by Manu Herbstein

Ama, a Story of the Atlantic Slave Trade
Brave Music of a Distant Drum
The Boy who Spat in Sargrenti's Eye
Ramseyer's Ghost
President Michelle or Ten Days that Shook the World

and

MANU HERBSTEIN

Copyright © 2009 Manu Herbstein
All rights reserved. This publication is protected by international copyright law. No part of this publication may be reproduced, stored in or introduced into any retrieval system, or transmitted, in any form, or by any means (electronic, mechanical, photocopying, recording or otherwise) without the prior written permission of the author.
The moral right of the author has been asserted.

First published in Ghana by Techmate Publishers, 2012
Edited by Helen Yitah
Burt Award for African literature, 2011

Cover image by Ben Agbee
Title text font: Vitamin by pizzadude.dk
West Africa map: ©dikobrazik/123rf
Ghana map: ©Rainier Lesniewski/123rf

This is a work of fiction.

ISBN 978-9988-2-4314-2

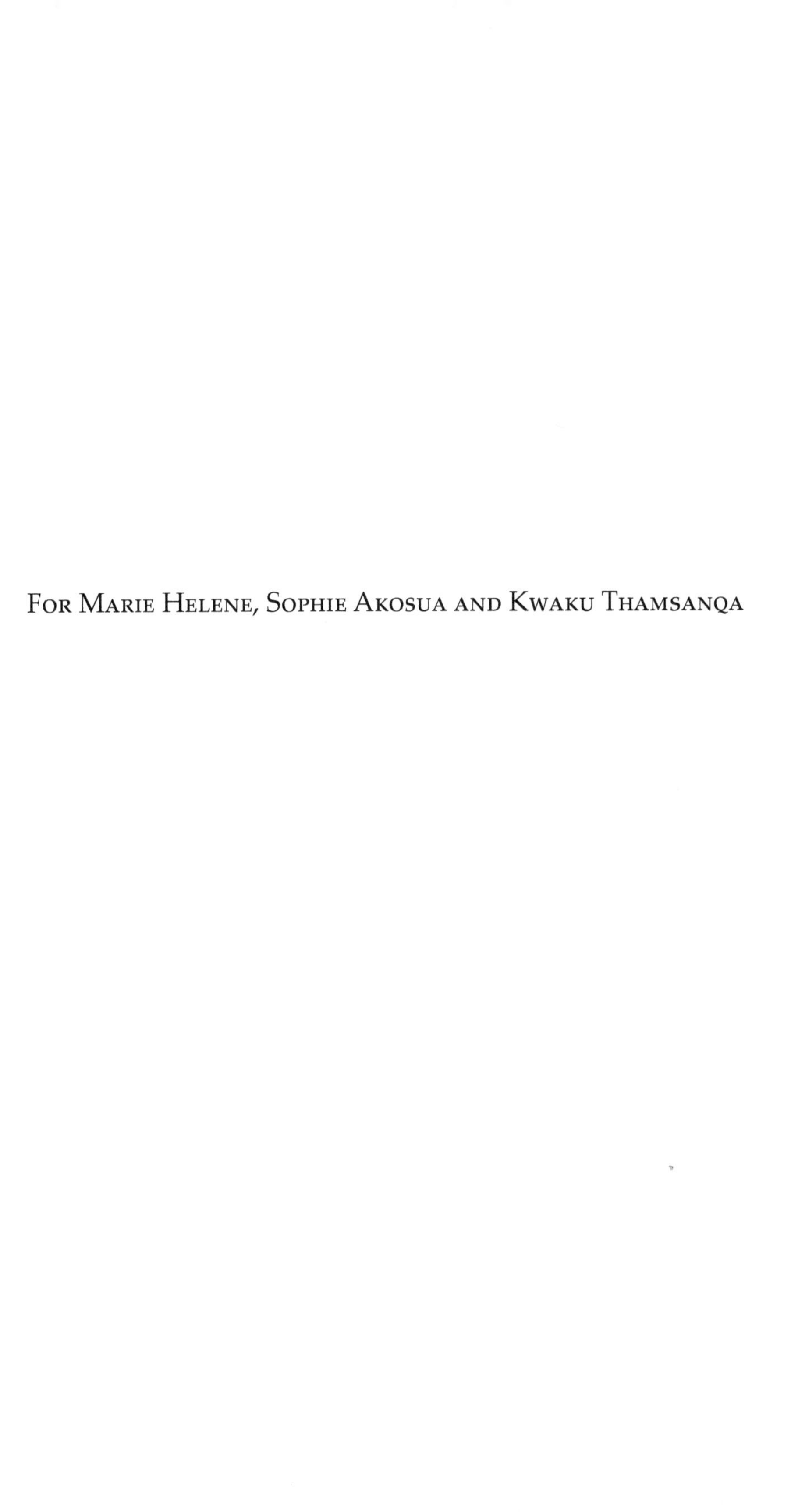

For Marie Helene, Sophie Akosua and Kwaku Thamsanqa

CHAPTER 1

Osman

English is not my mother tongue. I used to hate it. And even now that I've mastered it and made it work for me, I can't say that I have any love for it. Give me Hausa any day. Hausa is my mother tongue, though I have to say that it wasn't my mother's mother tongue. Does that sound strange? Try this, then. My mother's mother tongue was different from my father's mother tongue. So they had to compromise. When they first met the only language they had in common was Hausa, so that was what they spoke to one other. It's true that they both spoke a little pidgin English, but that is not a respectable language. After they began to live together in Accra as man and wife, they picked up just enough Ga and Twi to manage. Later, my father went to Adult Education to learn proper English, because without proper English there was no way he could sit the exam he needed to pass for promotion from Corporal to Sergeant.

We spoke Hausa at home. I can't remember either of them ever speaking to me in English or in their own mother tongues.

All my father ever told me of his background was the name of his village and that of the nearest town, Saboba. Once or twice, he went there. I think that must have been when his father died and then again when his mother died. But he didn't take us with him.

My father didn't encourage questions. Then he died and the answers to all my unasked questions died with him.

After my father passed away my mother also became ill, so ill that she could no longer go to the market. We were lucky that the Commander let us keep my father's room. He said that my mother should look for another place to stay but she didn't have the strength and he never did evict us. He said it was out of respect for my father, that he had been a good policeman, honest and respectful. When my mother was sick we had to survive on the small police pension and my father's social security. Even that was difficult, because the Social Security office wanted my mother to produce a document to prove that she had been married to my father, but she had no such document, because they never had been married. That was when I first realized how important it was for me to master English. If you can't speak good English those people in the Social Security office despise you. They give you forms to fill in, full of questions which you have no idea how to answer. Unless you know English, that is.

Hajia Zainab told me, "Osman, there is no way you can get on in this world, certainly in this country, unless you have made the English language your slave. Once you have done that you can make it do many things for you, things neither you nor I can even imagine now. I am a retired teacher, so I can help you. But the main job you will have to do your-self. Nobody is going to teach you what you are not willing to learn. There is only one way to master English and that is to read. Read, read, read. The road to your future is paved with books."

She signed me on at the Nima Children's Library. But that was later.

My sister Afia could read and write a little Arabic. My father thought girls shouldn't have too much education. So my mother used to take Afia to the market. When my father was still alive, the two of them would go together to the clinic at the Police Hospital every Monday in a police car, but when he died she had to take a taxi and I had to go with her because Afia wasn't much help. Some days, when my mother was feeling ill, she made me stay with her in our room. That was when I learned to cook. I was often absent from school at that time. My teacher thought I was playing truant and when I told him about my mother he accused me of telling lies. The boys whose parents were educated would send our teacher a note when their sons were absent, but my mother couldn't do that. My mother never learned to read and write; not in Hausa, certainly not in English, not even in her mother tongue. She was illiterate. It is hard to be illiterate. Nobody minds you.

At the end of the first term after my father died I failed my examination and had to repeat the class. As my mother's condition got worse, her medicines became more expensive and soon there was no money to pay my school fees. So I had to drop out of school.

I wasn't all that sorry because I didn't have good friends at that school. My classmates loved to tease me.

"Osman, what are you?" they would ask.

"I'm a Ghanaian," I would answer.

"Yes, we know that. We're all Ghanaians. But what are you?"

They wanted me to say that I was Dagomba or Frafra or Mossi or Kotokoli or whatever.

Once I asked my father what I was. He shut me up. It was only after he died and when I had to stay in our room with my mother that I began to understand why. My mother was a Dagomba, a "black" Dagbana, she told me. Her family were poor and she often went hungry. Then a man, a distant relative, offered to take her to Accra. He promised to find work for her. She would be able to send money back to her family. Her father agreed. The man put her to work as a porter, a *kayayo*, in the market and took all the money she earned, giving her just some small change for chop and soap. She had only one cloth and slept wherever she could find a place. When she was older she escaped from the man's clutches and moved to another market. She was scared that he would track her down but he never did and she never saw him again. Now, for the first time, she had some money of her own. She bought onions and put them on a head-tray and started trading. She told me that it was not easy but better than it had been when she first came to Accra. By that time she had lost all contact with her family.

One day a handsome young police constable spoke to her in Hausa. After that they would often meet. Then he invited her to his room at the Police Depot. She became pregnant. (That is, with me.) When her time came, she couldn't go back home, so she went and lived with my father. It was only then that she got to know that he was a Konkomba man. The Dagomba and the Konkomba hate each another. They never marry. Dagombas would think it shameful that a Konkomba man should have married one of their daughters. So my mother never thought of going home again and she didn't mix with the Dagombas in Accra because they might have asked embarrassing questions. In the same way, my father couldn't tell his people that he had married one of their enemies. They had only one more child, my sister Afia. They gave her that name because it means "the end of all problems" in Arabic. But it sounds like Afua, the name which the Akan give to girls born on Friday, so that is what people often called her.

There was only one bed in our room and my mother slept on it. Afia and I slept on mats on the floor. My first job every morning when I woke up was to take the bucket and go and fill it at the standpipe. It was only when I woke Afia to help me take the bucket from my head that I noticed something was wrong. My mother didn't respond to my morning greeting. I spoke to her again and then I shook her, but still she didn't respond. Then I went to call our neighbors, the wives of the policemen who lived in the rooms next to ours. They soon started wailing and in no time everyone on our floor knew that my mother was dead. They buried her the same day. We

Muslims don't keep the bodies of our dead in the mortuary for months like the Christians, who like to call their children from America for their funerals so that they can make a big collection to cover their costs and hope to make a profit.

They took Afia and me to the Commander's house. That was the first time I had been in a proper house. All our lives we had lived in just one room: my father, my mother, Afia and me.

The Commissioner's wife looked after us. She was a Christian. There was a big picture of Jesus Christ on the wall. I had learned about Jesus Christ in the madrassa. We Muslims honor him as a prophet but, unlike the Christians, we don't believe that he was the son of Allah. Anyway, the lady was kind to us. She gave us Fanta to drink. Then she sent two women sergeants with us to collect all our things from our room. All this time Afia was sobbing, quietly. I felt like crying too, but I didn't. When the Commander came home for his lunch, they went through my father's papers and then they talked about what to do with us.

"Osman," the Commander asked me, "did your father or your mother have any family in Accra?"

I didn't know how to answer and just shook my head.

"Speak, my boy," he said, "or don't you have a tongue?"

"Oh, Kwaku," his wife said, "don't be so harsh. They are bereaved. They must both be in a state of shock. Poor orphans, what are we going to do with them?"

"That is the question," said the Commander.

Then he called the constable who was on guard duty.

"Go and call the Imam," he said. "Tell him it's urgent."

The Imam is in charge of our mosque and of the madrassa where we go after school to learn Arabic and the holy Koran.

When he came they exchanged greetings: "Salaam Aleikum, Imam," and the reply, "Aleikum Salaam, Commander."

I stood up and made Afia stand up too.

"Imam, do you know these two children?"

"Of course," he said. "Some months ago I buried their father and this morning their mother, too."

Then he said a prayer to Allah for the souls of our parents.

"I need your advice," said the Commander. "They don't seem to have any family in Accra. I have examined their father's papers. It seems he has a brother in the North."

"Then that is where they should go," said the Imam.

Then he turned to me.

"Osman," he said, "Isn't that right? You and Afia must go to your uncle."

I was silent. My mind was in a turmoil. I didn't know any uncle. I had never been to the North. Accra was all I knew. I was close to tears. I looked at Afia but she didn't seem to understand. She was twelve years old but her English was not good.

"Right," said the Commander. "That's settled then. I'll send two of my men to take them."

I had to speak.

"Please, sir," I said, "I don't know any uncle. Please let me stay in Accra."

They looked at one another. Then the Commander asked his wife to take us to the kitchen and give us something to eat. While we were out of the room they decided our future. The Imam would make an appeal in the mosque on Friday for someone to offer to adopt us.

That's how I lost my only sister and got a new mother. Hajia Zainab volunteered to adopt me, but there were no offers for my sister.

Afia cried and cried, but there was nothing I could do. A woman police officer called Sergeant Fianko took her to our uncle in the North.

CHAPTER 2

Akosua

I adore my class teacher. Her name is Miss Priscilla Mensah. I think Priscilla is a beautiful name, as beautiful as its owner. My name is Akosua. How dull! One in every seven girls in Ghana is called Akosua. Except in the North, that is; and perhaps amongst the Ewes, too, and the Gas. But amongst us Akans, it's just seven names for girls and seven for boys. There are four girls called Akosua in my class, so Miss Mensah has to use our surnames to distinguish us. I am Akosua Annan. The other girls call me AA. When Miss Mensah calls me to the front of the class, they all whisper, "AA, AA," until she raises her eyes and stares them down, searching for the culprits. Then they pretend that they are concentrating on the open books on their desks. The cowards! And I? I put on my haughty look, raising my chin to display my lovely neck, challenging them all. "Teacher's pet," they'll tease me in the playground at break, but I won't mind them. No, that's wrong. Miss Mensah says that "don't mind them" is incorrect. It's Ghanaian English. The right expression is, "I will ignore them." Or perhaps, "I shall ignore them." Shall or will, will or shall, I never know which to use.

Priscilla is a beautiful name. It sings. And yet Miss Mensah hates it. She says it's a European name. At home, she says, nobody uses it. They call her Nana Yaa because she was born on Thursday, even though Yaa doesn't appear on her birth certificate.

"We should be proud of who and what we are," Miss Mensah says. "We are Ghanaians, Africans, African women. We are not Europeans. Our own names are perfectly adequate. Why do we have to borrow European ones? Is it because we nurture a secret wish to be Europeans, even second-class black Europeans?"

Miss Mensah spent some time in England. She went to University there and got a PhD. So we should really call her Dr. Mensah. I tried that once and she wagged a finger at me and then put that same finger to her lips. I guess she feels that calling herself Dr. Mensah would be seen as showing off. None of our other teachers has a PhD, not even our headmistress.

Miss Mensah has pretty lips, not too thick but not thin like those of Miss Jones who teaches us maths. Miss Jones is English. Miss Jones doesn't have a PhD, only a Masters. Miss Jones uses bright scarlet lipstick. Miss Mensah doesn't use lipstick at all, ever. She says the cosmetics industry is just another international conspiracy to rake in women's hard-earned money. And who do you think owns the cosmetic industries? she asks. And then she answers her own question: men, of course. Miss Mensah says our native cosmetics, like shea butter, are all she needs. No foreign chemicals for her. She says she was once persuaded to use a chemical hair straightener and once was enough. Never again, she says. Our plaited hairstyles are beautiful enough. Our problem, she says, is that we don't know how to recognize and appreciate what is our own.

But that's enough about dear Miss Mensah for now. I'll have more to say about her later; plenty more. But now it's time to say something about myself. I'm fourteen. I was born in March under the sign of Pisces, the fishes. Miss Mensah says astrology is a lot of superstitious tosh, but I have to say that is one issue on which we are not in agreement. It makes good sense to me that our characters should be influenced by the positions of the stars and the planets at the moment we are born. I researched Pisces on the Internet and this is what I found: we Pisceans are sensitive and imaginative, kind and compassionate, selfless and unworldly, intuitive (I like that) and sympathetic. Now that describes me precisely. Every one of those adjectives fits me like a glove and their accuracy only serves to support my belief in the scientific validity of astrology.

The Internet site also lists what it considers some bad characteristics of Pisceans. The first is that we are idealistic. Well, I don't think that idealism is a bad thing at all. Even if it were, I admit to being an idealist. Then it says we are secretive. Again, I don't see that as a negative trait. And it's true about me. There are plenty of gossips in my class—okro-mouths, we call them—who are quite incapable of keeping a secret. But I am certainly not one of them. You can trust me. All your secrets are safe with me. Cross my heart and hope to die!

Only the last four alleged Piscean characteristics don't fit me at all. I guess that they are the exceptions that prove the rule. (How can exceptions prove a rule, I wonder? I must remember to ask Miss Mensah about that in our next English class.)

Here they are.

Firstly, "escapist." Wrong! Not me at all. At all. On the contrary, I'm a realist.

Second accusation: "vague" Wrong again. I make a point of being precise. Miss Mensah sometimes accuses some of the other girls in my class of being vague and imprecise in their writing, but never me.

Numbers three and four: "weak-willed" and "easily led." Well, that's outrageous; almost enough to make me lose my faith in the scientific accuracy of astrology. I am certainly not weak-willed and definitely not easily led. How dare they suggest that? I must really write to the website to point out the error.

But enough about my character. Now, my appearance. I think I can say without fear of contradiction that I'm quite pretty. My hair is cut short since that is the rule of the school.

Only the girls in the senior class are allowed to let their hair grow long enough to be plaited. However, since my head has a good shape, short hair is not a disadvantage. Indeed, I've seen pictures of famous African models with close-cropped hairstyles in fashion magazines.

My lips are a little bigger than I'd like, but when the Big Bad Wolf told Little Red Riding Hood, "What big lips you have, my dear," what did she reply? "All the better to kiss you with, my dear," of course. My nose has a good African shape: broad, but not too broad. I think my eyes are one of my best features. The eyes are the gateway to a person's soul. I must have read that somewhere, not sure where. I spend time in front of the mirror practicing different expressions with my eyes. You know, curious, flirtatious, angry and so on. My neck is another good feature. Ghanaians admire a long neck and I have one.

As to my body, well, I'm still growing. Right now I'm somewhere in between skinny Geraldine Blankson and enormous, obese Ama Osei. (Sorry, Ama, I shouldn't have said that. I love you all the same.) I'm slim, but rounded in the right places. I've a good pair of legs, thank God. Although I'm not yet fifteen, when we go into town I can already see grown men giving me the eye. Not that I pay them and their dirty thoughts any attention. But I reckon that when I leave school at eighteen I'll be just about ready to enter the Miss Ghana Teen competition (and win!) and maybe do some professional modeling. There's a lot of money in modeling. I'm considering making a career of it. Oh my God! My parents would die of apoplexy! As for Dad and Mom, they have my life's trajectory all set out for me. First, a degree in law or medicine, something that can guarantee a good income, just in case of need. And then a good marriage, with children to follow. Heh! I'm not yet fifteen and still a virgin, and yet they have it all planned.

Dad and Mom. Well, I must be discreet; no dragging of family skeletons from musty cupboards and hanging them out on the washing line for all to see. Wow, is that a mixed metaphor! Miss Mensah says we must never mix our metaphors, but never mind. I like that image of the skeletons' bones rattling in the breeze. Talking of skeletons reminds me of how our Ashanti ancestors used to deal with their dead kings. First they would bury the deceased monarch, surrounded by the bodies of slaves they killed to accompany him to the next world and serve him there. They would allow a few years for his flesh to rot or be eaten by worms and then they'd dig up his skeleton. They'd clean the bones and drill small holes near the joints. Then they'd thread gold wire through the holes to hold the bones together. In the mausoleum at Bantama, each royal skeleton had a room of his own, where he (or it? what's the right pronoun for a skeleton, he or it?) where he would be seated on a chair. One room for Nana Osei Tutu, one for Nana Opoku Ware, I don't recall number three, one for Nana Osei Kwadwo and so on. I don't know whether number five, Nana Osei Kwame was given a place. He died in disgrace. I don't remember whether he was destooled for taking the Golden Stool with him on a trip to Mampong, or whether he was forced to commit suicide. Anyway, every year, at Odwira, the living Asantehene would go to Bantama and deliver food and drink to his predecessors in office and ask their spirits for their advice and blessing. You won't find those details in any of our textbooks but I can assure you they're true. I found them in a book in the University library. That's one advantage of having a parent who's a professor. Indeed, two parents in my case.

One day I told this story to Geraldine Blankson. We were working together on our history homework. She listened to me without saying a word, her eyes growing bigger and bigger all the time until they were like saucers.

When I finished, she asked me, "Have you finished?" and when I answered in the affirmative, she exploded. Exploded, I tell you, like a bomb or a hand grenade.

"Haven't I always told you," she said, "that you Ashantis are uncivilized savages?"

Geraldine is a Fanti. The Fantis think that they are more refined than the rest of us. We think they're all jokers, not serious about anything except, for the men, wearing suit and tie, and for the women, wearing ridiculous hats to church. Of course Cape Coast, where our school is, is the Fanti capital. Every Fanti, even one who was born in a remote village in the bush, will claim a home in Cape Coast.

Geraldine continued, "Let me teach you a bit of Ashanti history. In 1869 you people went raiding for slaves and happened to capture the Reverend Ramseyer of blessed memory. After letting his baby son die of hunger and sunstroke, you kept Mr. and Mrs. Ramseyer under house arrest in Kumasi for four years. That gave you a wonderful opportunity to open your eyes and ears to the word of God for the first time. But you were stubborn. You continued to worship your pagan fetishes and practice human sacrifice. The only Ashanti man who listened to Ramseyer's message was Prince Owusu-Ansah, and that was only because he had received his education here in Cape Coast. In 1874 the British stormed Kumasi and punished you by razing it to the ground. They were doing God's work, but you still refused to get the message. So, in 1896 the British had to go in again and finish the job. The best thing they did was to exile your King Prempeh to the Seychelles. Ramseyer settled in Kumasi again, to give you a second chance. But again you would not listen. The good word went in one ear and out the other. It wasn't until Prempeh returned in 1925, by that time having seen the error of his former ways and become an Anglican, that you people started going to church. That is why you are so backward. We Fantis had more than a hundred years' start on you when it came to education."

I let her go on, just showing her through my eyes the contempt I had for her distorted version of history. Unfortunately I didn't have the facts at hand to contradict it. But one thing I remembered Dad telling me.

"You forgot something," I said.

Having let off all her steam, she was somewhat deflated now.

"What?" she asked.

"In 1896 the British terrorists stayed in Kumasi for just five days. Lord Baden-Powell, the man who founded the Boy

Scouts, was there. He took great delight in blowing up our Royal Mausoleum at Bantama with dynamite and looting all our golden treasures. He was your terrorist par excellence. Just ask Miss Mensah about him."

"Well, she would say that, wouldn't she?" said Geraldine. "After all she's an Ashanti herself, isn't she?"

"And you're a Girl Guide, aren't you?"

We let it rest there. Geraldine and I are friends. Hearing us argue and insult one another, you wouldn't believe it, but we are. Rivals too, though. Last year I beat her at English and History. This year she's determined to turn the tables on me, just to prove that Fantis have better brains than we Ashanti have. Just let her try. Of course she's jealous of me; and it's not only my brain-power that she's jealous of. Her main problem is her flat chest. And she doesn't hide her concern. In the shower she has been heard to say, "Oh my dear little titties, what have I done to you that you refuse to grow?" And it's not only her tits. No hips. Just like a boy. I'm sorry for her, Geraldine Blankson, in spite of the fact that she's such a tribalist.

CHAPTER 3

Osman

The Imam brought my new mother to the Commander's house straight after Friday prayers. I recognized her. She was one of the women who had visited my mother when she was ill. The one bag of rice and one bag of beans they brought lasted us a whole month.

They came in a car with a driver. I saw them come. My new mother sat in the back with the Imam. The car belongs to her. It is an old ivory-colored Nissan Bluebird, about twenty years old, but the driver, Amadu, keeps it clean inside and polished outside.

"Osman," she said, "I'm your new mother. The first thing we have to decide is what you should call me. What did you call your mother who has just left us?"

"Please, madam, I called her Umma," I said.

Umma is one of the Hausa names for mother.

"Well," she said, "that will always be her name in your memory. My name is Zainab. I am called Hajia Zainab, because I have been on the Haj, the pilgrimage to Mecca. But I don't need to tell you that, do I? You have been going to the madrassa and the Imam tells me that you're a good student. Well now, names. I think you had better call me Mama. How about that? Will that suit you?"

I said, "Yes, Madame."

She laughed.

"Say, 'Yes, Mama.'"

I said it and she laughed again.

"For the time being you'll keep your name, Osman Said. Later you can make up your own mind whether you want to take my surname."

I liked my new mother but she was still a stranger. It took me a little while to get used to calling her Mama, but now I don't give it a second thought.

Mama has her own house at Roman Ridge. I have a room all to myself with a bed and a desk and chair. The house has two bathrooms; one is for Mama and one is for me, for me alone. When Mama's real children, who are grown up and live abroad, come to Ghana for their holidays I'll have to share my bathroom with them and one of the grandsons will share my bedroom. Mama says I'm his uncle now, though he's older than I am.

The bathroom has a shower, with separate taps for hot and cold water. Mama had to show me how to use them and the WC. When I first moved in she used to inspect the bathroom every day to see that I was keeping it clean, but now she only has a look at the weekend.

Over the next few weeks Mama told me the story of her life, not in order, mind you, but in bits and pieces. I had to put them together like the jigsaw puzzle she gave me to play with. Mama is a Fanti. She grew up in Cape Coast. Her parents were Christians, Methodists. Her father worked in the government and her mother was a trader in Kotokoraba Market. After she finished Middle School she went to Teacher Training College. There she met a fellow student who wanted to marry her. Her father objected because the man was a Muslim. She married him all the same and converted to Islam. It was the right decision. He was a good husband. When her first son was born her father repented and came to the outdooring. Her husband soon left the teaching profession and went into business, dealing in motor spare parts. She continued teaching and before she retired she was the headmistress of a primary school in Accra.

Something was puzzling me.

"Mama, do they speak Hausa in Cape Coast?" I asked.

She laughed. She seemed to like the questions I asked her, so I started to think of new questions, just to make her happy.

"Some traders there speak Hausa," she said, "but not many. No, I only learned Hausa when I came to live in Accra. Everyone in Nima and Maamobi speaks Hausa, so it wasn't too difficult."

They had two children, a son and a daughter. The son trained as a doctor. Then he went to America for further studies. He's married to an American lady and they have two children, Mama's grandchildren. She often speaks to them on the telephone. She said I should speak to them too but I was shy and didn't know what to say.

When I first went to stay with Mama I didn't know how to use the telephone. She taught me how to answer properly.

Now when the telephone rings I pick it up and say "Hajia Zainab's residence. Osman speaking. How may I help you?"

We keep a pen and a notebook right by the telephone. If Mama is not in, I write down the name and number of the caller and his message. Or her message, because many of the callers are ladies. Nobody has called me yet. If my uncle in Saboba had a telephone I could speak to Afia, but I'm not sure whether they have telephones in the North.

Mama told Amadu, her driver, to teach me how to use her mobile phone. Now I'm an expert. Whenever she has a problem with it, she no longer asks Amadu; I am the one she asks for help. She has promised me that one day I'll have my own mobile phone but she says I'll have to earn it and she hasn't told me how.

Hajia Zainab is not poor but she's not all that rich. She has a pension from her time as a school teacher and though at Eid her son and her daughter in America send her some money, she still has to trade to make ends meet. She has a small store on the Nima Highway where she sells auto spare parts. She inherited the shop from her husband when he died.

Once I was settled in Mama's house and knew the rules and we had got to know one another better, my education was next. What with my father's death and my mother's illness, I had lost a whole year. When I went to live with Mama the school year had already started. Mama is a member of the board of governors at the Maamobi Boys High School, so she thought there would be no problem getting me registered there. But the headmaster said his school was full and that I would have to wait until the next term. He checked with all the other Junior High Schools nearby and everywhere the story was the same. She didn't like to leave me alone in the house so she took me to her store every day.

I quickly learned the names of the spare parts in the store: spark plugs, bearings, brake linings, shock absorbers, carburettors, all new, imported from Japan. Mama had just bought a computer and there was a man working there, a consultant he was called, listing all the stock and the prices and putting them into the computer's memory. We had one computer at my old school but I never got a chance to use it. This time it was just me and the consultant. And Mama, of course. The consultant was training her.

I was enjoying myself but at the back of my mind I was worried. I wanted to get back to school.

One day Mama was chatting to a customer. His name is Master Zarifou and he is a master auto mechanic at S. K. Anani's Engineering Works. It is Master Zarifou, Mama says, who has kept her Bluebird running smoothly for so long. And if ever her car breaks down in town, she only has to call him on his mobile phone and he'll send a senior apprentice or even come himself to sort out the problem.

Mama was telling Master Zarifou about the trouble she was having getting me into school.

Master Zarifou said to me, "Osman, how old are you?"

I said, "Please sir, I'm fifteen."

At first Master Zarifou said nothing. I could see he was thinking. Then he spoke.

"Madame," he said, "if you like, and if Osman likes, he can join my apprentices until the school is ready to take him. He would learn something practical about internal combustion engines. And because he would only be coming for two or three months, I wouldn't charge you. What do you think?"

And so it was agreed that I would spend every morning, Monday to Saturday, at S. K. Anani's Engineering Works and every afternoon at the shop except Friday afternoon when Master Zarifou took me with him and the other Muslim apprentices to the mosque. Because of the store Mama didn't always go to prayers on Friday and when she did, she usually went to the mosque on the other side of town, where she had met my mother Umma.

In the beginning I thought about my mother Umma every day, especially when I woke up, but I had a new mother now and a new life was opening for me and so I thought about her less and less.

When I reached Mama's store after my first day as an apprentice, I found that she had made space in a small room at the back for a table with a reading lamp. She had persuaded the headmaster to let her have copies of all the school books for the time I had missed.

"Osman's private study," she said.

Sometimes she called it, "Operation Teach Yourself," other times, "Operation Catch-Up."

Every afternoon she would set me a task; call it school work or call it home work. And before Amadu drove us home in the evening, she would correct my mistakes and explain anything that I didn't understand. Since she had been a teacher, it was easy for her. For me, it was not so easy. In school, you sit there, forty of you, two to a desk, waiting for your teacher to decide what to teach you. Sometimes the teacher is off sick, or is attending to some private business that will fetch him more money in a day than his teacher's salary will give him in a month. Or perhaps he is a day late in returning from the funeral he traveled to over the weekend. On such days we learn nothing. And even when the teacher is present, his attention is divided among forty children.

Now, from two o'clock to five o'clock every day there was no teacher, just me, alone. I had to be my own teacher. I had to learn from the books. Mama would poke her head in for a minute or two in between customers, but that was all. I managed to pack more into those three months than all I had missed in the two difficult years before. I was determined that when the headmaster tested me he would put me in the senior JHS class where I belonged.

Mama's store was closed on Sunday.

"Sunday is the Christians' day of rest," she said, "but we are not Christians, are we?"

Sunday was my time for reading. Mama registered me at the Osu Children's Library. Every Saturday, I would go there to hand in my old books and take new ones. They let me take three at a time. I would usually select two story books and one from the shelves marked "non-fiction." The only time Mama allowed me to watch television was when there was a big football match. Otherwise, no television.

Mama spent Sunday cooking for the next week. She would allow the cooked food to cool and then pack it into small plastic boxes, labeled "Joloff Rice" or "Palm Soup" or "Nkontommere" or whatever and put them in the freezer. They had to have labels because it's difficult to distinguish one kind of frozen food from another. When we came home from work she would take out a box, put the frozen block of food into a special glass dish and put it in the microwave cooker. In a few minutes it would not only be thawed but heated up and ready to eat. Magic! We would eat together and then I would do the washing up. Sunday was also laundry day, but since Mama has a washing machine, all I had to do was to hang the washed clothes on the line and, later, do the ironing. There was still plenty of time for reading.

Mama quoted a Hausa proverb which her late husband had taught her.

"*Karatu, farkonka madaci, karshenka zuma.*"

It means that study is difficult but the rewards are great.

"Once you go back to school and make some new friends," she said, "you'll have time for play as well as study. But right now it's books, books, books. The road to your future is paved with books."

At the same time I was learning all sorts of different things at the workshop.

CHAPTER 4

Akosua

"By the time you're my age," said Miss Mensah, "you'll have forgotten practically everything you are going to learn in the next two years."

Geraldine put up her hand.

"Please, Miss, I'm Geraldine Blankson. Please Miss, if what you said is right, what's the point?"

"The point, Geraldine, is to separate the worthy from the unworthy. The worthy will receive a certificate which will entitle them to proceed to a university where, in due course, if they are diligent, they will receive another certificate. The unworthy, if they are girls, will look for a job which doesn't require too much brain power while they keep their eyes open for a suitable husband. What our educational system fails to do, Geraldine, is to give you an education. Over the next two years, I am going to do my level best to do just that: give you an education."

We are in Form 2, with two years to go until we take our SHS exams. We do ten subjects, six core and four elective. Miss Mensah is our elective Literature in English teacher. And this term she is also teaching us elective History because our regular teacher is on maternity leave.

"We have six periods a week together," Miss Mensah told us, "three for Literature and three for History. Five of those should be enough to cover your syllabus. In the sixth period … well, you'll just have to wait and see."

There are thirty in our class. To each of us she handed an A4 sheet with about forty names printed on it in alphabetical order of the surnames.

"Please print your own name and the date at the top of the page," she said. "Then put a tick next to each printed name that you recognize. Be honest. I might ask you to stand up and tell the class what you know about the persons whose names you've ticked. Right, you have three minutes. Go!"

Ama Ata Aidoo, Ghanaian writer; Yaa Asantewaa, Ashanti queen mother, no problem; Jane Austen, English writer. Then I ticked these names: Charlotte Brontë, Cleopatra, Queen Elizabeth the First, Anne Frank, Joan of Arc. Heh, I thought, all of these are women. What's this all about? Miriam Makeba, Winnie Mandela, of course I know them. Efua Sutherland, another Ghanaian writer, Florence Nightingale, Ellen Johnson Sirleaf, President of Liberia, Queen Victoria, Oprah Winfrey.

"OK," said Miss Mensah, "now count how many you have ticked and write the number at the bottom of the page. Then pass the papers to the front, please."

I had ticked fifteen. Fifteen out of forty six. If this was an exam, I would surely have failed. But, fortunately, it wasn't an exam. Akosua Annan is not used to failing exams.

This is Miss Mensah's list. See how many names you recognize. No cheating, mind

"This," said Miss Mensah, "is a somewhat arbitrary list of great women, some greater than others, of course, and one or two of them, in my opinion at least, rather nasty characters. An educated Ghanaian woman should be able to recognize practically every one of those names."

We giggled.

The next thing she did was to call us up to the front of the class, one by one, by name. This was our first session with her and she had met none of us before that day. That must have

Ama Ata Aidoo	Frida Kahlo
Louisa May Alcott	Rosa Luxemburg
Maya Angelou	Miriam Makeba
Yaa Asantewaa	Winnie Mandela
Jane Austen	Carson McCullers
Simone de Beauvoir	Marilyn Monroe
Aphra Behn	Toni Morrison
Margaret Bourke-White	Florence Nightingale
Sarah Bowdich	Mbande Nzinga
Charlotte Brontë	Emmeline Pankhurst
Rachel Carson	Rosa Parks
Cleopatra	Nawal el Saadawi
Marie Curie	Olive Schreiner
Amma Darko	Ellen Johnson Sirleaf
Angela Davis	Harriet Beecher Stowe
Queen Elizabeth I	Efua Sutherland
George Elliot	Margaret Thatcher
Anne Frank	Harriet Tubman
Rosalind Franklin	Queen Victoria
Indira Gandhi	Alice Walker
Dorothy Crowfoot Hodgkin	Oprah Winfrey
Zora Neale Hurston	Mary Wollstonecraft
Joan of Arc	Virginia Woolf

been why she'd made us write our names on the papers. Clever Miss Mensah.

I was sitting in the front row so my paper was on top.

"Akosua Annan," she said, and I saw her matching name to face for future reference. "Akosua Annan, fifteen ticks, not bad."

Then she showed us a little cloth bag and explained that it contained one folded piece of paper for each name on the list.

"Akosua, put your hand into the bag and take one.

"Who did you get?"

"Sarah Bowdich," I replied. "Never heard of her."

When the rest of the class had followed suit, she said, "What I want each of you to do during the next couple of weeks is to research the woman whose name you have drawn. You may not find much information in the school library, but there is always the Internet. No cut and paste, please. This exercise is not for marks. It has two objectives. The first is to introduce you to research methods. The second is for you thirty young women to link up with thirty other women who have done great things in one way or another. I want you to write a short critical essay, with a portrait of your subject if you can find one. Who was this woman? What were the challenges she faced in her life and what success did she have in dealing with them? Do you think we should remember her (if she is dead) or celebrate her (if she is still with us), and if so, why?"

She said we should send our essays to her by e-mail and promised to circulate them. The writers of the first three she received would be rewarded with an invitation to read their essays in class.

"If they're any good, and I'm sure they will be, we might publish them on the school web-site. Then we'll make time, perhaps over a weekend, to discuss our findings."

There were still a dozen or so women in her little bag, or at least their names were. She offered them to us but there were no takers. I thought about it but decided against it. I was going to have my work cut out if I wanted to discover anything about this unknown woman, Sarah-What's-her-name.

Then the bell rang. As we filed out of the class, chattering as we always do, Miss Mensah called me aside.

"Akosua," she said. "You drew one of the most obscure names. After her husband died Sarah Bowdich was known as Sarah Lee. See what you can find and then come and talk to me. I have some rare material about her which you might not find on the Internet."

"Yes, Miss, thank you, Miss," was all I could think to reply.

Outside, under the mango tree where we often sit during break, the girls were all talking at the same time.

After lights out that night I lay and thought about Miss Mensah and how lucky we were to have such a charming and clever woman to teach us. We generally give our new teachers a hard time, but she seemed to have won our hearts without really trying. And then I had a great idea. I would add one more name to the list: Miss Mensah's. I had heard my father talking about Chairman Mao's Little Red Book and Colonel Gaddafi's Little Green Book. I would make a note of Miss Mensah's wise words and record them in a Little Blue Book. Why blue, when it's usually pink for a girl and blue for a boy? Miss Mensah, I thought, has the mind of a man. And then I fell asleep.

This is what I read to the class a week later.

Sarah Wallis was born in England in the year 1791. Little is known about her early life until, at the age of 22, she married Thomas Edward Bowdich, who was about the same age. She must have just had her first child, or still been pregnant, when her new husband left for Cape Coast. That's right, our very own Cape Coast. Mr. Bowdich was employed by the African Company of Merchants which was based in the Castle. Note that in spite of the name, those merchants were all Europeans. His job description was "writer." In those days all letters were written with quill and ink and copies also had to be written out. I guess that means that he was a clerk or a secretary. He had got the job through his uncle, Mr. John Hope Smith, who was a senior official in the Castle and later became the Governor. Today we might call that nepotism.

Sarah, who according to the English custom of the times, was now known as Mrs. Thomas Edward Bowdich, must have got fed up waiting for Mr. Thomas Edward Bowdich to fetch her, so she went to the port of Liverpool with her baby daughter and looked for a ship, a sailing ship, of course, bound for Cape Coast. When she couldn't find one she decided to go instead to Freetown in Sierra Leone where the English had set up a sort of colony for freed slaves. There were twenty-six men on the ship, including the captain and one other passenger, and a whole lot of live ducks and chickens and the like to provide them with food on the long voyage. Sarah was the only woman on board. I wonder how she managed. I mean for privacy. I guess that the toilet facilities on the ship must have been pretty primitive. And how often did she get to take a bath? There is no way of knowing.

A Royal Navy ship of the anti-slave trade patrol took her from Freetown to Cape Coast. When she got there (or should I say "when she got here"?) she found that her beloved Thomas Edward had left for England. Her trip from Liverpool to Cape Coast had taken three months. She must have been even more thoroughly fed up when she arrived to meet Mr. Bowdich's absence, as we say. It was lucky for her that Mr. Hope Smith was around to look after her. He was stationed at Anomabu so she went and stayed with him there.

After Mr. Bowdich returned to Cape Coast he was sent on a mission to Kumasi. That was in 1817. He was away a long time, so again Sarah was on her own. Sadly, their baby daughter died while he was away. The nature of malaria was unknown at that time and the cause of the child's death is given merely as "fever." In those days the Gold Coast was known as the White Man's Grave. In Kumasi Mr. Bowdich made Ashanti friends and subjected them to a barrage of questions about Ashanti history and culture and religion. He made drawings of the most important buildings in the city and kept detailed notes of all he saw and heard. While he was there the Asantehene, Nana Osei Bonsu, made him the gift of a girl whose name he gives as Adua. I guess she was called Adwoa, a Monday born. The British had made the slave trade illegal in 1807, so this transaction puzzles me. Mr. Bowdich also "collected" a number of gold objects which are still in the British Museum in London.

In February, 1818, Mr. and Mrs. Bowdich left Cape Coast to return to England. It seems that they took Adwoa and a 16-year old boy with them as servants. Their ship had to head south first, to Gabon, to load a cargo of timber and to catch the south-east trade winds. Sarah writes that while they were on board, the fair copy of Mr. Bowdich's book, *Mission from Cape Coast to Ashantee*, was written. At least one modern authority thinks that she is likely to have helped her husband in writing this work. During their return voyage pirates from a Spanish slaving vessel boarded their ship. Sarah writes that their "black servant-girl," presumably Adwoa, cried bitterly, "for she fancied she should be again forced into slavery," but all the pirates stole was the ship's stock of food, leaving them to face near starvation before they reached England.

After the publication of Mr. Bowdich's book the couple moved to Paris where they studied with the French scientist Baron George Cuvier. They both learned Arabic and Sarah became a skilled artist, specializing in scientific illustrations.

In 1822 the couple set off on another voyage to Africa. They took their two small children with them. Due to poor winds, they missed a connecting passage at the island of Madeira and had to wait there for fifteen months. Sarah had another baby there. In all she had five children of whom three survived. They eventually reached Bathurst (Banjul) in the Gambia, but just six weeks after their arrival Mr. Bowdich died of fever.

An obituary to Mr. Bowdich had this to say of Sarah: "Mrs. Bowdich was the companion of his travels, the sharer of all his perils, nor less the ardent participator of all his hopes, and in her affectionate arms he breathed his last. Herself endowed with every accomplishment that could render her the worthy associate of such a spirit, she entered with enthusiasm into all his views, and assisted with her talents many of the most scientific of his operations. Nor is there a living pen better qualified than hers to do justice to his memory."

Sarah was now a widow with three infant children and no resources to call upon except her knowledge and her talents. She supported herself and her children from the meager income she earned from her scientific writing and illustrating. Over the next ten years she published, in installments, *The Freshwater Fishes of Great Britain*. Each installment had four printed illustrations. Since color printing had not yet been invented, she added color to every single print using water paints and gold and silver foil.

This is a print of one of her pictures of a fish. (I held it up for all to see. There were gasps of admiration.)

Then, in 1825, Sarah was invited to contribute a story to a Christmas annual called *Forget-Me-Not*. (An annual was a book containing entertaining stories and pictures, published once a year to be given as a Christmas present.)

Her first story, *Adumissa* (whom she has a Cape Coast man describe in pidgin as one "who pass all woman handsome that black man ever saw … men die for her—they like her too much") was so successful that it started her on a new career as a writer of short stories.

The next year she wrote *Amba, the Witch's Daughter* to expose "the barbarous feeling which exists in great force against supposed witches, in all the parts of Africa which I have visited."

Her third story, *The Booroom Slave*, fascinates me. It tells the story of Inna, the bright but spoiled teenage daughter of a Bron chief who ventures alone into the forest near her home and is captured by agents of a vengeful rejected elderly suitor. Inna's brother Kobara and his friend, Inna's fiancé, Miensa, search for her but in vain. She is taken to Cape Coast to be sold but escapes and tries to find her way home, avoiding human contact for fear of re-enslavement. Paddling upriver in a stolen canoe, she encounters a party of whites, led by (I guess) Mr. Bowdich, who delivers her to an "English female," the narrator of the story. The narrator in due course teaches Inna English and some of the skills appropriate to a maid in a middle class English home. She also promises Inna that if she accepts the Christian God, He will see to it that she returns to her family. In due course Kobara and Miensa arrive in Cape Coast on a trading mission and Inna is re-united with them. They take her home to Bron, where she and Miensa live happily ever after. It's like a fairy tale.

Sarah tells us that "The history of *The Booroom Slave* is taken from the narrative of a girl who came from that country, and waited upon me: from her lips were many of the details noted, and to them nothing has been added but what is in strict consonance with the scenes spoken of, and of their inhabitants." That girl might well have been Adwoa, Nana Mensa Bonsu's gift to Mr. Bowdich. The Bowdich's took the real Adwoa to England with them but what happened to her there is a mystery.

The Booroom Slave was republished in 1835 in a collection of Sarah's writings entitled *Stories of Strange Lands*. In her introduction to this book Sarah claims that "… every story is founded on truth; every description of scenery, manners and customs, has been taken from life," and "as much of the language of the actors has been preserved as is consistent with civilized ears."

Sarah died in 1856 at the age of 65. An obituary in the *Literary Gazette* said that "she was beloved by all who knew her. Her talents she used unweariedly, unselfishly. Her spirit was oppressed by no pride of intellect or vanity. She bore up like a heroine under burdens which would have prostrated most women, and all from a natural impulse of love and duty."

I've told you who Sarah Wallis-Bowdich-Lee was and described some of the challenges she faced in her life and how she met them. At a time when the English treated their women as second-class citizens, she was a successful explorer, scientist, writer and story-teller. Although she wasn't one of us, I mean she wasn't a Ghanaian or even an African, she was here, right here in Cape Coast, nearly two hundred years ago. I think we should recall her from obscurity and honor her memory.

I'd practiced reading this. It took me about ten minutes. Too long, I thought. They'll be bored and start fidgeting. But when I finished they started clapping. I was astonished. Then Geraldine stood up, still clapping. Ama Osei followed and then all the rest of the class. They gave me a standing ovation. It made me feel so good, especially when Miss Mensah also stood up clapping.

Ama Osei was next. She had drawn Queen Elizabeth, the Virgin Queen. I guess that what we were all interested in was the virgin part but Ama didn't go into that. She won a polite round of applause.

Third was Geraldine. Her famous woman was Maya Angelou, an African-American writer who lived in Ghana in the time of Kwame Nkrumah, our first president, and wrote about her experiences in a book called *All God's Children Need Traveling Shoes*.

I don't know much about those times and since Miss Mensah said that there was a copy of Ms. Angelou's book in our school library, I have decided to borrow it. Geraldine says that at the age of 83 the lady is still alive and still writing. Perhaps we should invite her to pay us another visit before she dies. Just a thought.

"All three of you have done an excellent job," Miss Mensah said, "but there is more to do. I don't want you to treat these women as heroines, at least not until you have persuaded yourselves that they deserve that title. These are some of the questions I'd like you to ask about each of your subjects: What sort of society (or societies) did she live in? Sarah Bowdich lived most of her life in England but she also lived in France and right here in the Gold Coast. Maya Angelou lived in Egypt and in Ghana before returning to the United States of America. So, ask yourself, how did women fit into each of these societies? How did your woman relate to the men in her life? Was she free to develop all her talents? What connection, if any, did she have with Africa? What can we learn from studying her life? Is her life relevant to your own? If so, how?"

"Now it so happens, quite by chance, that each of our first three women has a connection to the theme we're going to tackle next month, which is the Atlantic Slave Trade. Queen Elizabeth the First of England had her dirty fingers in the pie right at the outset, profiting from her investments in the slave trading missions of the notorious pirate Captain John Hawkins; Sarah Bowdich lived in Cape Coast Castle just ten years after the last slave was sold there; and Maya Angelou is the descendant of enslaved Africans who might well have been shipped from our own shores. Think about them when we deal with the Atlantic Slave Trade in our history classes and when we visit Cape Coast Castle next month."

CHAPTER 5

Osman

Mama takes me to the workshop on the first day. It's not a tidy place, just a small yard, I guess about 40 paces long by 20 paces wide, that is if you could find a straight path to pace it out. It's packed tight with private cars, taxis, pickups and tro-tros. I count them: forty-five four-wheelers and a motorbike. There is an old blue Land Rover with a white roof and a Peugeot "one pound, one pound," but most of the vehicles are Japanese. One Honda has four flat tires and looks like an abandoned orphan. Maybe the owner brought it for repair and found the estimate beyond his means. One of the yellow taxis has the words "Dirty Enviness" painted on the dirty back window. I wonder what made the owner choose that name.

Master Zarifou hasn't come to work yet, but his senior apprentice, Mohammed, welcomes Mama and then some of the other masters come too: Malam Salam, the master auto electrician, Master Yao, the gas welder and panel beater and Master Yakubu, the spray painter. Malam Salam is first and he speaks to Mama in Hausa, but when Master Yao joins them, they change to English. Master Yao is an Ewe and doesn't understand Hausa well. After Malam Salam has asked after Mama's health and about her children overseas, he asks whether she has some problem with her Bluebird. She starts explaining about me but just then Master Zarifou arrives. The traffic delayed him. He tells Mohammed to take charge of me and to introduce me to the other apprentices.

The apprentices are all much older than I am. Mohammed is nearly thirty, almost an old man already, though he isn't married yet. He had his graduation party last year so I don't know why he is still called an apprentice. He is from Burkina Faso and used to work in Ivory Coast but there was a war there and so he came to Ghana.

The youngest, except for me, is Kateb, who is eighteen. He grew up in Kumasi. His father is a driver and his mother sells yams. His home language is Hausa so we are free with one another. He tells me that in Kumasi he was accused of bad behavior with girls and playing truant. So he was sent to stay with his married sister in Maamobi.

Faisal Hassan is a Kotokoli like Master Zarifou and is the only apprentice with proper overalls. He was born in Accra but when he was five his parents took him to Kano in Nigeria. Last year they both died and he had to come back to his grandparents in Accra. He speaks Nigerian Hausa. It is different from ours, but close enough for us to understand one another. I tell him that my parents also died recently and that makes us friends.

I shake hands with all the apprentices and try to remember their names and match them to their faces: Baqir, Ibrahim, Hado, Kibsa and some more. There are eleven in all. I am the twelfth, though I don't intend to serve my term. When I tell them I'm planning to go back to school, they're jealous. All of them say that they had to leave school after JHS because their parents couldn't afford the fees, but I'm not sure whether I should believe them. Everyone knows how difficult it is for children in the khaki-khaki schools to get into Senior High School, fees or no fees.

Most of them are dressed in old tee-shirts, dirty with oil and grease. Their going-home clothes hang on a line at the back. On Kibsa's shirt I read "ROWING TEAM IC MLXXXI World

Champions." I am puzzled. What do the words mean and how do you pronounce them? I ask Kibsa but he has no idea. All he says is, "*Obroni wawu*." That is what we call second-hand clothes. It is a sort of joke: it means "the white man is dead." I write the tee-shirt words in my secret notebook. Maybe Mama will know what they mean. I like to read the writing on tee-shirts and the back windows of taxis.

Mohammed is still doing the introductions when Mama calls me back. It is already past the usual opening time for her store.

"Osman," she says, "there has been a change of plan. Master Salam has made a good suggestion. You'll spend three weeks with Master Zarifou, then Master Salam will take you for another three weeks and after that you'll be with Master Yao until it's time for school. And when Master Yakubu has a car to spray, you'll go and help him. That way you'll be a Jack of All the Trades they practice in this yard. And even if you go on one day to become a Medical Doctor and learn to treat the illnesses of human beings, you'll always remember what you've learned here from these car doctors."

Mama likes a joke. They all laugh.

When she leaves I have a good look round. There is only one entrance to the yard, a narrow roadway full of potholes. Every car has to enter or leave by this road. Apart from the entrance all four sides are shut in by buildings. Two sides face the back walls of single story courtyard houses. The wooden shutters of their windows are always closed as if the residents won't like what they'll see if they open them. On the left side there's a three-story concrete building, unfinished. Later I ask the watchman for permission to climb to the top to get a bird's eye view of our yard. If I had a camera I would take a photograph. The watchman says that the owner died and there is a dispute in his family about the inheritance.

"Even if they 'gree, na money short for finish," he says.

He tells me that every month he has to fight them for his wages, and then he sucks his teeth.

I think then, "Inheritance. My father left me nothing except my name and his good reputation, and if that hasn't already been forgotten, it soon will be."

On the front side of the yard, facing a rough road, there is a row of single-story shops, built of concrete with rusty iron rods projecting from the flat roof. Master Zarifou sees me looking at the shops: one selling cement, one selling plywood, one empty.

"That belongs to our landlord," he says. "Before it was built it was part of our yard, but he thought he would make more money by building the shops. Now we pay the same rent for half the space."

Master Zarifou and the watchman, both telling me things that aren't my business.

Inside the yard, there are two trees, one at each end; outside, next to the road, there is a big mango tree with its roots exposed by the rain. That is where the masters sit and chat when they have no customers.

Against the back wall there is a row of offices, built with wooden posts supporting rusty corrugated iron roofs and walls of weathered Wawa boards. Two signs read, "Malam Salam – Auto Elect – Battery Charging" and "A to Z General Upholstery Stuffing Car-roofing Furniture." Cylinder head gaskets, like the ones Mama sells, hang on nails. Outside Master Yao's office there are oxygen and acetylene bottles and one of his apprentices is using the gases to repair the underside of an old car. Master Salam has a television in the lean-to outside his office, next to the battery charger. When the work isn't too much he switches it on for the big football matches.

The roofs have some leaks. When it rains, we sit in the customers' cars.

I need to urinate, so I ask Kateb where I should go. He says I have a choice between the public toilet down the street and the back wall of the shops. In Mama's house I have a bathroom all to myself. At the police barracks there were communal bathrooms. In this yard there must be twenty or thirty masters and apprentices and they don't even have a urinal.

While I am with Master Zarifou, Mohammed is my teacher.

He makes me repeat the names of all the tools, like spanners and screw drivers. When he is lying on his back under a car he calls out, "Osman, number twelve flat spanner," and I pass it to him. He teaches me the difference between petrol and diesel engines. I learn about the carburettor, which mixes petrol and air, and the distributor which sends electricity to the spark plugs. Mohammed has removed the cylinder head of an old Toyota. He turns the crank shaft by hand so I can see how the pistons move up and down.

The apprentices talk mainly about two things. The first is their work. They discuss every car, what is wrong with it and what needs to be done to fix it. I learn just by listening to them. Sometimes Master Zarifou joins this kind of conversation.

Their second subject is girls. All of Master Zarifou's apprentices are Muslims but some are better Muslims than others. The good Muslims say that talking about girls, even thinking about girls, is sinful and that you should try to drive sinful thoughts out of your mind by praying to Allah. But when the others, bad Muslims according to the good Muslims, talk about the girls they know and what they have done with them, I can see that even the good Muslims listen.

Mama warned me when I joined her that I should have nothing to do with girls.

"There will be plenty of time for that when you've finished your education," she said.

I'm confused. The apprentices are all older than I am. I never say anything when they talk this kind of talk, but I do listen. And at night, in my bed, the stories the boys tell come into my head. I try to drive them out by praying, but it doesn't work. I think that the Devil is putting those thoughts into my mind, and often the Devil is too strong for me to overcome. At last I fall asleep, but the Devil is still at work and he sends those bad thoughts about girls into my dreams. And then I wake up and my sleeping cloth is wet.

I tell Faisal about my problem. He laughs.

"When I was your age I was the same," he says, "until I found out that it has nothing to do with the Devil. It happens to all boys. It is part of becoming a man. That sticky stuff that comes out of your penis has seeds in it. When you get married you will put your thing inside your wife and plant the seed inside her and a baby will grow from it."

I know some of this from the biology class at school, but it doesn't solve my problem. Then he tells me what to do so that I can sleep without being disturbed by wet dreams. It works but I am still worried that what he has taught me to do is a sin and that Allah will punish me.

"Don't worry," Faisal tells me. "All the boys do it. That is how Allah made us. In the time of the Prophet, peace be upon him, boys and girls would get married when they were young. Today, how will a poor apprentice like me find a wife? Even our senior, Mohammed, who is nearly thirty years old, doesn't have the money to pay for a wife. The bad ones get a girlfriend and do what married people do without getting married. Now that is a sin."

"Have you done that?" I ask him.

"None of your business," he says.

Master Yakubu, the Master Auto Sprayer, doesn't have a spraying booth of his own, so when he has a spraying job to do, he hires a booth for a day or two. On other days he just hangs around the yard waiting for a customer. His sister and her husband have a container nearby which they use for dressmaking and tailoring. Master Yakubu sits chatting with them while they work and while his small son Adeeb and his little daughter Aisha play. Aisha is three and very pretty. Adeeb is about five. They are my friends.

One day Master Yakubu takes me with him. Before the spraying, we have to sand down the rusty patches until the metal underneath shines. Then we use masking tape and old newspapers to cover the windows and the handles so that they don't get painted. I soon learn to do this. The actual spraying is more difficult. You have to keep the spray gun moving at the right speed. If you move too slowly, the paint runs and leaves ugly drip marks. If you move too fast, the finish quality is poor. Master Yakubu lets me try, but not on his customer's car. The paint is costly so I have to learn mainly by watching rather than by doing.

While we are working, Yakubu asks me about my family. Then he tells me his own story. His family is from Aniho in Togo but his father was born in Koforidua. He started school at Wenchi, on the other side of the country, where his grandfather was working as a driver and his father was a carpenter in the Public Works Department. When he left school his grandfather taught him to drive a truck and employed him as his mate. Then he came to Accra to learn auto spraying as an apprentice.

Yakubu was once a Roman Catholic. So was his first wife. They had only one daughter. She is married and attending Teacher Training College. In Nima, where they were living, all their neighbors were Muslims. Yakubu had a dream which made him decide to convert to Islam. His wife's family objected and persuaded her to leave him.

His second wife was born in Ghana but her family comes from a country called Benin, on the other side of Togo, before you reach Nigeria. At home they speak Hausa. Because Yakubu was already an adult when he became a Muslim, he can't read Arabic. He just knows the prayers by heart.

One day, after I had gone back to school, Mama and I had to make a trip to the North. She had the Bluebird overhauled and Master Zarifou said he guaranteed that it could make the trip without trouble as long as Amadu kept to the main roads and didn't take short cuts. Mama said it would be hot in the North and decided to have the Bluebird's air-conditioning fixed. I went with her to the yard. I wanted to go and greet my old friends but she said I should wait while she discussed the matter with Master Joshua Nkansah, the yard's Car Refrigeration Master, also known as "Cool." There are three Christian Masters in the yard. Master Cool is one of them. It took quite a long time for Mama and him to start talking about the Bluebird. That was because they were exchanging gossip about their grown-up children who are abroad.

Master Cool has two sons in America. One is studying to be a doctor and the other is taking a degree that will make him a master of architecture. He has another son in Germany, also studying to be a doctor and married to a German lady, a white woman. I've seen plenty of whites of course. Some of them are customers at the yard and at Mama's store, but I've never spoken to one. I wonder what it would be like to be married to a white woman.

My days at the yard pass quickly. Soon it is time for me to go back to school. Master Zarifou says I have to have a graduation party. So Mama hires plastic chairs with 'Gye Nyame' written on them and buys seven crates of minerals and forty cartons of take-away chicken. We meet in the road by the mango tree. The masters make speeches and they make me an honorary master. Honorary means I'm not a proper master—that takes three years at least, and I've been here less than three months. At the end they all call out, "Speech, speech," and I have to stand up. At first I'm shy. I thank everyone by name and then I list all the things I've learned. At the end I thank Mama for her good thought in sending me to the yard. When I finish they all clap. Then Master Zarifou stands up and the rest of them do the same, still clapping their hands. That is what is called a standing ovation. I read it in a book.

CHAPTER 6

Akosua

"Today," said Miss Mensah, "we're going to start a series of discussions about a matter that I suspect might be on your minds and close to your hearts. Any ideas about what that might be?"

"Exams," said one of the girls.

Miss Mensah pulled a face.

"Much more important than exams," she said.

Geraldine put up her hand.

"Yes, Geraldine," said Miss Mensah, but before my poor friend had a chance to open her mouth, Lily Mends in the back row called out, "Small tits."

Lily is the wit of our class. Not much good when it comes to exams but always quick off the mark with a funny comment. That was a cruel one. Everyone in the class knew about Geraldine's concern about the delayed development of her mammary glands. Cruel, yes, but funny. Everyone laughed. Me, too. Even Miss Mensah had to screw up her face to suppress an involuntary grin. Geraldine turned round and fired a laser beam of hatred towards Lily. Lily blew her a kiss.

"Geraldine," said Miss Mensah, "pay no attention to that vulgar and uncalled for remark. And rest assured that Mother Nature will in her own good time make adequate compensation for her dilatory behavior."

Wow! Miss Mensah certainly knows how to use the English language.

"Now, Geraldine," said Miss Mensah, "what were you about to say when you were so rudely interrupted?"

Lily Mends had bruised her feelings and Geraldine was sulking.

"I forget," she said.

In other circumstances Miss Mensah would have visited her own caustic wit upon my friend, but now she just said, "Class?"

Hands went up all over but some of the girls couldn't wait. There must have been at least five simultaneous replies: "Boys."

Miss Mensah smiled.

"Boys. Men. The male of the species. Homo sapiens. Which, in case you don't know, is the Latin for Wise Man. Note: Wise Man which in this sense must include Woman. As usual, we of the female sex are something of an afterthought.

"Who knows who coined the term Homo Sapiens?"

Only one hand went up. There was a note of surprise in Miss Mensah's voice.

"Yes, Lily," she said.

"If it's Latin, Miss, it must have been Julius Caesar," said Lily.

"Good try," said Miss Mensah, "but Julius Caesar wasn't the only person who spoke Latin."

She then gave us a mini-lecture about how the Latin language spread throughout Europe and spawned, from West to East, Portuguese, Spanish, French, Italian, Romanian and probably a few others.

"The term Homo Sapiens, my dear Lily Mends, was coined, not by Julius Caesar, who died in the year 44 BCE, but by the Swedish botanist, zoologist and medical doctor, Carl Linnaeus, some two and a half centuries ago. Look up Homo Sapiens in Wikipedia and you'll be directed to 'Human.' Well worth a read. Indeed, I now set that for your homework: read Wikipedia on what it means to be Human."

"OK, let's get back on course. Boys. On your minds and, for some of you, perhaps, in your hearts. Is that unanimous? Shall we talk about boys? Any objections?"

I turned round to look at Charity Baah and her fellow born-agains in the third row, but their faces were blank. They didn't know what they were letting themselves in for.

"As usual," said Miss Mensah, "I'll try my best not to lecture you. Well, not too much. This subject is as broad as a boy's shoulders so I'm going to break it down. I'll set the theme for the day and give you a brief introduction. Then the floor will be open. You may find some of what I'll be saying controversial, perhaps even offensive. Just bring your critical female minds to bear on it and speak out.

"Today our theme is 'The Human Being is an Animal' and we'll consider what bearing this statement has on relationships between the male and the female of our species."

Then the lecture started.

"All animal species," she said, "except the simplest, reproduce by sex. The female produces an egg, the male produces a multitude of sperms. One of these tiny sperms succeeds in penetrating the egg and initiates the beautiful, mysterious process which in due course results in a new creature which will, in its turn, share the responsibility for the continuing existence of its species. In most species, including our fellow mammals, nature provides a key which sets this process in motion. When a female dog, for instance, has eggs ready to be fertilized, we say she goes on heat. She sends out odors which the sensitive noses of all the male dogs in the district detect. I guess you will have observed what happens next.

"We humans are somewhat different. We have devised means to keep the propagation of our species under control, more or less. For one thing, unlike dogs, we generally conduct our sexual activities in private. Moreover, we recognize that the sexual act between male and female, man and woman, has at least one purpose other than the production of babies. By its secret pleasurable intimacy, it has the power to strengthen the bonds of love between a couple. Any questions?"

Harriet Koomson put up her hand. Harriet always seems to be half asleep, so we call her Dreamy Harriet.

"Please, Miss," said Harriet, "Have you ever been in love?"

"Yes, Harriet," said Miss Mensah, "I have. And maybe I still am. However, I don't intend to discuss my affairs of the heart with you. And while we're on the subject, I think I'll lay down a set of rules for these sessions. Respect one another's privacy. No gossip. Treat what I say, and what you say in the discussion which I expect will follow, as totally confidential. Agreed?"

The class agreed. Miss Mensah continued.

"We'll talk more about love in another session. Right now I want to talk about the male as an animal. But first, a short word about girls. With girls, I have no need to tell you, the onset of puberty is marked by our first period. This may be accompanied by some pain and, if you have not been forewarned, by considerable embarrassment and even mental anguish. It is not generally accompanied by sexual pleasure.

"Now boys. With boys, the onset of puberty is marked by a wet dream."

She paused. Miss Mensah is a good actor. She knows how to vary the pace and volume of her speech for the best effect.

"OK," she said. "Any volunteers? What's a wet dream?"

There was a lot of shifting around and giggling. I guess we all knew the answer but we didn't have the right words to express it.

"Lily Mends?" said Miss Mensah.

I guess she was punishing Lily for the way she had embarrassed Geraldine, but for once, Lily had a straight answer.

"Nocturnal emission," she said.

Miss Mensah nodded.

"From puberty," she said, "and throughout their lives, male humans produce in their testicles a sticky fluid called semen. The semen is populated by large numbers of sperms, so small that they are invisible to the naked eye. Now the semen can't just go on accumulating—the body has to get rid of it. Nature intends it to be injected into a woman's womb so that a sperm can fertilize an egg. But our young sleeping boy is not ready to do that. Instead, he has an erotic dream, on the content of which I permit you to speculate, and the fantastical performance in his mind leads to an erection. Action in the dream results in ejaculation of a charge of semen. If he doesn't wake up right away, the next morning our boy finds his pajamas and sheet wet and sticky, much to his embarrassment."

She held up her hand to stop the titters (no pun intended!)

"Later, our boy may learn the pleasures of masturbation, assisted by erotic day dreams. Shall I ask Lily to define masturbation for us? No, I'll spare her. Stroking his organ with his hand gives our boy pleasure and leads to an erection and then to a discharge of semen. The wet dreams may become less frequent. Or they may not. I really don't know.

"Well I expect all this is not news to you. Some of you have brothers and eavesdrop on their talk. Some of you may have discussed this amongst yourselves. A few of you might even have enlightened parents who have taught you the facts of life.

"What I want you to understand is the biological reality. The build up of semen and the pressure to get rid of it exists in all healthy men, even Catholic priests who have sworn vows of chastity. Without it our species would cease to exist. For most men the most pleasurable way to get rid of their semen is by sexual intercourse with a woman. If this is done within a loving relationship, it is also a pleasurable experience for most women."

She paused and seemed to be running her eyes over ours, left to right, right to left, row by row. Then she continued:

"The problem for the female in this relationship, is that if no precautions are taken, an egg may be fertilized, causing the woman to become pregnant. I said: problem. If the intercourse takes place within a stable relationship and if the woman wants to have a baby and if the male partner accepts his responsibility as a father, fine. There may be problems— poverty, for instance—but they are shared. In most other circumstances it will be the woman who bears the brunt of the problems. Any questions? Harriet? Lily? Ama Osei? You haven't said a word."

There were no questions. We were all absorbed. I guess none of us had ever heard talk like this before, at least not from an adult.

"Let's list some of the potential problems.

"Case 1. The boy and girl are both young, perhaps as young as you are. Neither of them is emotionally or economically ready to be a parent.

"Case 1A. Never having discussed sex with their parents, they both feel guilty. The boy persuades the girl to have an abortion. This might cause her permanent physical damage and it will certainly cause her mental trauma. Their relationship is likely to be ruined. The boy gets off scot-free. It's the girl that bears the pain.

"Case 1B. The pregnant girl summons up her courage and confides in her mother. A family meeting decides that she will have the child which will be looked after by the girl's mother or grandmother. Her education is interrupted, perhaps for good. The girl's family approaches the boy's family and demands compensation. Marriage is out of the question. The boy is too young. But he is not too old to get a good beating. The relationship is unlikely to survive all this unpleasantness. A baby girl is born. Will she in turn become another teenage mother?

"Case 2. The girl is young but her sexual partner is an adult, perhaps a fairly young married man, maybe a teacher, even one of her teachers. Or he might be older; old enough to be her father, or even her grandfather. A sugar daddy. In every case the man has a near monopoly of power. The power is usually economic, the power to give gifts of money, clothes, a new pair of shoes, time spent in his comfortable love nest, being driven in his Mercedes or BMW. If it's a teacher, it might just be the power to give enough marks to pass an exam, or even to win a scholarship. If the girl is vain, she might be won over by no more than the power of sweet words. He loves her. He's going to divorce his wife and marry her. The stupid girl succumbs to flattery; she believes him.

"You might expect the man, being older and more experienced, to take precautions, to use a condom. But many men dislike using condoms. They say it's like taking a bath with your socks on. What happens in this case if the girl gets pregnant? The man will do everything in his power to keep her quiet, perhaps to force her to have an abortion. Another life damaged, if not ruined. And what prospects are there for the baby? It would take a brave girl to name and blame the baby's father. The rascal has had his fun. He does a disappearing act."

There was a whole lot of rueful head-shaking in the class. I thought, "I'll never let that happen to me," and I guess most of the other girls were thinking the same.

"So far I've only spoken of unplanned pregnancies. Another serious danger is infection with an STD, a sexually transmitted disease, a venereal disease. The most common ones affecting teenage girls are Chlamydia, Gonorrhea, Syphilis, Trichomonas vaginalis and Herpes. More Latin, by the way. All over the world hundreds of thousands of young people are infected with these diseases every day. For some reason girls are twice as vulnerable as boys. They are all nasty; I mean the diseases and their symptoms, not the boys; and they all need immediate medical attention; that does include the boys. The long-term consequences of failure to treat these diseases can be frightening.

Should you ever experience symptoms which make you suspect that you have been infected with an STD, you will almost certainly suffer from shame. Bury your shame and go and see a doctor. At once. Do not delay. And take the male animal who might have infected you along with you, even if he says he has no symptoms. But best of all, just avoid the risk of getting infected.

"And then there is HIV/AIDS, for which there is as yet no cure. We might talk about that in another session.

"Right now, before I open the floor for questions and discussion I want to burn just one thought into your minds. In all your relationships with boys, with men, guard your own identity. You may find it expedient to humor your partner's sense that their sex is stronger and cleverer than ours, but in your inner consciousness, keep control. Be subtle, be diplomatic, but if you want your loving relationship to endure, you must be the manager. OK. Any questions?"

I recall only one of the questions. It was the one which I asked.

"Miss, which do you think is better: separate schools for girls and boys, or mixed schools, like Ghana National?"

Trust me to open my big mouth. Miss Mensah decided that that was an issue we should debate.

Since I had raised the question, she appointed me the proposer. The motion was "Mixed schools are better than single-gender schools." To my horror, she nominated Charity Baah as my seconder.

Lily Mends was appointed the opposer of the motion, with Geraldine as her seconder.

At break we took our customary places at the wooden picnic table under the mango tree: Geraldine, Ama and I.

"Chief mischief maker," said Geraldine.

"Who?" asked Ama.

"Miss Mensah, of course. Making me team up with nasty Lily Mends."

"And me with Chastity, I mean, Charity," I said.

Behind her back we call her Chastity Baah because she's always preaching abstinence from sex. She's a Christian fanatic, a fundamentalist, not my favorite person.

"It makes you think, though," said Geraldine.

"Think what?" asked Ama.

"About giving up your virginity," said Geraldine, "I mean, it's so risky. Getting pregnant would be bad enough, but just thinking of those Latin diseases gives me the shivers."

"You're beginning to sound like Chastity Baah," I said. "As for me, I have it all planned. I'll be in control, just like Miss Mensah advises. No condom, no sex. But first I have to find the love of my life."

Ama said nothing.

I did a lot of studying, thinking, planning for that first debate and, even if I say so myself, my presentation was first class. Lily Mends' opposing arguments were quite shallow but her presentation was brilliant and she had the class laughing. Charity was useless as my seconder. She just couldn't keep to the subject. Geraldine was excellent. After contributions from the floor of the house, we voted. Our side lost, just. But then Miss Mensah called for a second vote, for the best speaker, and I came out tops.

From then on we had regular debates, at least once a month. The topics were usually controversial. Pornography should be banned. Prostitution should be made legal. Topics like that. Capital punishment was another. Then we went public. Miss Mensah persuaded the headmistress to set up a debating society. Here, the topics were less contentious, sometimes even boring. But that was good training. I learned how to make a dull subject interesting. I abandoned my plans to be a model and decided to do law and then go into politics.

I often teamed up with Lily Mends. I was good at the serious stuff: research, statistics, arguments. Lily could make a joke out of anything. So we complemented each other. Then we went national. But that's another story.

CHAPTER 7

Osman

A week before the next term started, Mama took me to the school, the Maamobi Boys' Junior High School. Because of the afternoons I'd spent in my study in the storeroom behind Mama's shop and the library books I'd been reading, I had no trouble passing the placement test. The headmaster congratulated me and put me in the senior JHS class. I'd made up for most of the school time I'd lost while my mother was so ill. Mama gave me a hug and told me, "Well done." It was the first time she had done that. I was shy and didn't know what to do. I don't remember my mother ever hugging me like that.

The boys in the class had been together for a least a term and had made their friends. There was only one other new boy in the class, a Christian Fanti called Jackson Brew. He asked me to be his friend. As for me I'd never had a Fanti friend before, let alone a Christian, so I hesitated.

When I told Mama about Jackson, she said, "Osman, don't you know I am a Fanti and that I was born and brought up a Christian? You are too narrow-minded. You must learn to select your friends from the whole human race. But just boys, mind you. Not girls, not yet. You are still too young for that. There will be plenty of time for girls later."

I didn't argue with her but it was not as easy as she made it out to be. At least I was in a boys' school so there were no girls in the class to distract me.

On the second day the headmaster brought a man and a woman to our class. He told us they were from Family Planning and that they were going to give us Sex Education. Some of the boys in the class must have been twenty already. They were dunces but they had stayed on in the hope of getting their BECE certificates. One way or another they were probably going to end up unemployed. When the head made his announcement, one of these boys started cheering, "Yeah, yeah," and clapping and some of his friends started to laugh.

The head pointed to them, one by one: "You, and you, stand up," he told them. Then, "Go to my office and wait for me outside the door."

"They'll get six of the best," Jackson whispered to me. We were sharing a desk.

The head must have heard, but by the time he turned round, Jackson had dropped his eyes and was concentrating on the open book in front of him.

The Sex Education man talked about the male anatomy and about puberty and hormones and the woman told us about the female anatomy. Then they took turns in telling us why it was bad to have sex before marriage. One of the worst things a boy can do is to impregnate a girl—that means to make her pregnant.

"If your girlfriend got pregnant, could you support her?" the woman asked. "Boys don't have babies, only girls. It is a shameful, cowardly thing to make a girl pregnant and then run away from your responsibilities. If she is still in school, that might be the end of her education. If you have a sister, just think how you would feel if a boy did that to her."

The other bad thing is disease. If one partner has a disease, called STD or Sexually Transmitted Disease, the other one will almost certainly catch it. That is, if they have sex.

The man told us what can happen to you if you get STDs like syphilis or gonorrhea. That shook us into complete silence.

Worst of all is HIV/AIDS because, so far, they haven't found a cure for that one. He went on and on about AIDS and the class began to fidget. There was just too much to remember. Some of it was interesting but there were many long new words.

The woman took over.

"Statistics tell us," she said, "that some of you will choose to ignore all the good advice we have given you so far. The advice I am going to give you now, you will disregard at your peril. Disregard it and you might end up being infected by HIV and dying young."

Then she took a wooden model from their bag and used it to demonstrate how to use a condom.

The class tittered but she gave us a look which silenced us.

"Do not misunderstand me," she said. "I am not telling you to have sex before you are married; on the contrary. But if you decide to ignore my advice and allow your animal instincts, your lust, to overcome good sense, then at least protect your future and that of your unfortunate partner."

"Any questions?" she asked.

One of the boys stood up.

"Sir and madam," he said. "I respect you as my elders but what you have told us is bad. I am a Muslim. It is a sin for Muslims to have sexual intercourse outside of marriage. That is what the Holy Prophet, peace be upon him, told us. It is written in the Koran. I can quote you the shura if you like. What you are doing is wicked. Also, I respect the lady, but she should not be present when such things are discussed, let alone do a demonstration as she has just done. That is the business of men. The lady should talk to girls and the gentleman should talk to boys."

That might have started a long argument but just then the bell rang.

After school that day Jackson asked me, "How did you find it?"

"Find what?"

"The Sex Education, of course."

I didn't know what to say so I asked him, "How did you find it?"

That's just what he wanted. He wasn't really interested in what I thought. He wanted to tell me what he thought.

"Rubbish," he said. "I know more about sex than the two of them put together."

I wanted to ask him whether he had ever been with a girl but I was scared he would say yes and then what would I say?

"Would you like to have some real Sex Education?" he asked me.

I hesitated and he took that for a yes. I don't think Jackson could imagine me saying no.

Then he asked me, "Have you got some money?"

"Money? For what?"

"For some real Sex Education," he said. "Just five cedis will get us half an hour."

That's how I ended up in a special private room at the Gye Nyame Internet Café. In the main room there were ten computers. On the wall a notice said, "419 AND PORNOGRAPHY STRICTLY FORBIDDEN."

Jackson said something to the man behind the counter and handed over my five cedi note. I regret, I regret. I should never have given him the money. The man gave him a key. Jackson knew his way. He unlocked a door. Inside there was just one computer with a big screen. Jackson turned the key.

"Do not disturb," he said to the door.

I had heard people talking about the Internet but I didn't know much about it. Not so Jackson. He was an expert. He pressed keys on the keyboard and pictures of naked women, mainly white, appeared on the screen, one after the other, some of them as young as me. One notice on the screen read, "All the actors in this website are guaranteed to be eighteen or older." Then there were men, mostly a bit older, but not much. That's all I can say. I can't tell all the details.

Jackson clicked a key to see how much time he had left.

"Now watch this," he said.

This time it wasn't a still picture, it was a movie. I admit it: I was fascinated. I had never seen anything like it. I tried to look away, to pray, but the images were too powerful.

It was what Jackson did next, and what he said, that brought me to my senses. He shocked me so much that I picked up my school bag, unlocked the door and ran out, leaving the door open. I ran all the way home.

After that, Jackson never spoke to me again.

But he had done his evil work, the work of Iblis, the Devil. At night, every night, as I tried to fall asleep, Iblis would send those images into my mind. I would fight to expel them; I would recite passages from the Koran, but to no avail. Iblis was too strong.

Our Social Studies teacher was Mr. Kojo Smith. He was fresh out of Teacher Training College and new to the school.

"The past performance of this school in the BECE has been atrocious," he told us. "Shameful. But that is the past. My target for this year is 100% success."

There were murmurs in the class.

"I hear you," he said. "You don't believe it's possible. Well, I'm going to do my best to prove you wrong."

He held up some papers in his left hand.

"This," he said, "is the Social Studies syllabus."

"And these," he continued, holding up some more papers in his right hand, "are past exam papers."

"I have carried out a detailed study of the syllabus and I have analyzed every exam question over the past five years. In History, for instance, most of the questions are multiple choice. Here is an example," he said, reading from one of the papers. "In what year was the Atlantic Slave Trade abolished? You have five options: 1807, 1957, 1907, 1700, 2007."

He wrote the dates on the blackboard.

"Who knows the right answer?"

I was sitting near the back of the class. I put up my hand. I was the only one. He nodded to me.

"1807," I said.

He was surprised.

"Correct," he said.

Then he asked me my name.

"How did you know the answer? Did you guess?" he asked.

"No, sir," I replied.

"How then?"

"I read it in a book, sir," I said.

"What book?" he asked.

" It's called 'A History of West Africa,'" I said. "I found it in the Osu Library."

"Aha!" said Mr. Smith, "It seems we have a scholar amongst us. A *krakye*."

The class laughed. It was as if he were mocking me for getting the right answer. At that moment I decided never again to put my hand up when he asked a question.

"That is not how we'll reach our target," he said. "I know that I can't expect you to read library books to pass your exams. What I do expect is that you will read the set books, or at least those parts that have a direct connection with the syllabus and the exam questions you can expect."

His system, he told us, was to get us to memorize all the important dates and names and events in the syllabus. Our job, he said, was to get the maximum number of answers correct without guessing.

After school that day the older boys in the class, the dunces, jeered at me, calling me *krakye*. I ran all the way to Mama's shop. She was serving a customer. I went in to the back room, threw my school bag down and put my head on my desk and cried.

"Osman," Mama said, "what's the matter, my boy?"

I didn't want to tell her but she insisted.

"That's outrageous," she said. "I'll take it up with the headmaster tomorrow."

"Mama," I said, "I beg you, that would only make it worse."

It took some persuading to get her to agree with me.

From then on I kept my head down in Mr. Smith's class, handed in my homework on time and did my best to learn his foolproof system of passing the BECE. He soon forgot that I existed.

CHAPTER 8

Akosua

When we arrived at the reception area of the Castle there was already another group there: boys! No need to guess where they came from—their green tee-shirts proudly proclaimed the name of their school in Accra. It wasn't one of the better known ones. In fact, I'd never heard of it before. The one grown man among them, no doubt their teacher, was deep in conversation with another who turned out to be our tour guide. He beckoned to Miss Mensah and she joined them.

The guide clapped for silence.

"Ladies and gentlemen," he said.

One of the boys said, "Yeah."

"Joker," I thought. "He's probably the dunce of his class."

"Welcome," the guide continued when the laughter subsided. "My name is Isaac Mainoo, and I will be your guide this morning. I have just been telling your teachers that we expect two coach loads of tourists to arrive shortly. Because of that our time is limited and I have persuaded them to let me take you round in a single group. I trust that this will be the beginning of a long and loving relationship between your two schools."

Loving! Another joker! There was a buzz of comments. Miss Mensah and the boys' teacher smiled at each another.

"On a more serious note," Mr. Mainoo went on, "during the tour, I plan to subject you to a short experience intended to help you understand the state of mind of the enslaved Ghanaians who passed through this place. The effect can be traumatic. It should be, to achieve its purpose. In the past some visitors have found it beyond their emotional capacity to handle this experience. Some have fainted; some have burst into tears. So, before we start the tour I always warn our guests of the danger. In due course I will give you the opportunity to opt out of this short part of our tour. If you have any concerns, please do just that, opt out. To the rest of you, I beg, please don't mock those who choose not to join us.

"One other issue. The slave trade is serious business. Any levity on your part would be singularly inappropriate. I reserve the right to ask any jokers amongst you to leave the tour and return to the reception. Understood? On the other hand, I will give you plenty of opportunity to ask questions. OK, let's go."

This is not the place to repeat what Mr. Mainoo told us about the history of the slave trade and the castle. We all had to write about that in our class essays; and there is much more in books and on the Internet. I just want to describe what I experienced inside the dungeon. It wasn't quite what I had expected from Mr. Mainoo's warning.

You enter the dungeon by going down a steep ramp. Above you there is an arched roof lit by just one dim electric light. There is a single small opening, about the size of a shoe-box, high up on one wall. The walls are dank, the floor somehow disgusting.

Mr. Mainoo introduced two assistants, each holding one end of a rope.

"At night," he said, "no light enters through that little window up there, so we've installed a shutter to turn day into night. When I switch off the electric light, you will be in complete darkness, as the slaves were. Using their rope, my assistants are now going to herd you into a corner so that you can experience the congestion that the slaves would have had to endure while they were incarcerated in this terrible place. I'm going to leave you in this state for just two minutes. Please observe complete silence and try to summon up in your minds the spirits of the slaves who spent not minutes, but months, in this dungeon over two hundred years ago. Treat their memory with respect. Understand that some of them might have been your own distant relatives. And just one more thing. I shouldn't have to say this but it's not all that long ago that I was a teenager myself. Boys! Respect the girls. Keep your hands to yourselves, please!"

That drew some embarrassed laughter, perhaps from the very boys who might have been planning to take advantage of the darkness. Then the shutter snapped down and the light went out. The rope forced us back into a corner, tightly packed, one against the other. Observing Mr. Mainoo's rule of silence, we couldn't even whisper to one another. Bodies pressed into me on all sides. It was pretty unpleasant. There was no way I could know whether I was surrounded by boys or girls. I seemed to have lost all privacy. I had become an object, a thing, dehumanized, humiliated. I tried to call up the spirit of an ancient unknown slave relative, a girl like me, perhaps.

I was distracted by a growing pressure on my right hip. I tried to move away, but we were packed tight. There was no escape. Boys! They are like animals, unable to control themselves. Those 120 seconds dragged on and on and on. There seemed to be no end. I thought of crying out for help, but then I remembered that Mr. Mainoo had given us the chance to opt out of this experience. And it was an experience. Something I shall never forget. Before this, slavery and the slave trade had been remote, like the colonialism and imperialism that Miss Mensah is always talking about. But now I was learning to identify with those African slaves of old. I had become, briefly, a commodity to be bought and sold in the market.

Mr. Mainoo interrupted these thoughts.

"I am going to switch on the lights," he said, "but before

I do so, I want you to raise your right hand and send it searching for another. When the lights go on, keep your grip and speak to the owner of that hand. If he or she is a stranger, introduce yourself. As the rope is removed and your freedom of movement is restored to you, talk to one another. Exchange views on what you have just experienced."

After the darkness and the silence, the noise was like an explosion. There was the excitement of finding out who your partner was. It was like a party game, or wondering what would be printed on the card in a Christmas cracker. Now I have to make an admission. I sent my hand searching in the direction of that boy, you know, the one who was pressing against me in the dark. Naughty me! But I was curious. Miss Mensah says that curiosity is a good thing; a driving force in the development of mankind, she says (or words to that effect).

The boy was about my height, perhaps a bit shorter, quite good-looking. Involuntarily I dropped my eyes. "I'm called Akosua," I said, "Akosua Annan."

He looked down too. He seemed to be shy.

"I'm Osman," he said, "Osman Said, from Maamobi Boys High School in Accra."

I already knew the name of his school from his tee-shirt.

"Are you a Muslim?" I asked.

He looked me straight in the eye now. I thought I detected a glint of anger at my question.

"Yes," he said. "And you? Are you a Christian?"

"Well, sort of," I said. "My parents are Christians but I'm something of a free-thinker, like my teacher, Miss Mensah."

As soon as I said that, I realized that I'd made a mistake.

"A free-thinker?" he asked. "What's that?"

"Never mind," I said. "Maybe we can talk about that some other time. Right now we're supposed to be discussing the experience we've just had. What do you think? What was going through your mind during the darkness and the silence?"

That was naughty of me but it just came out. I guess I wondered whether he had been thinking with his head, his heart or something else. I need to discipline my own thinking.

"I was thinking," he said, "that most of the slaves came from the North. Like me. Well, actually, I was born and grew up in Accra, but my parents came from the North. And you, what were you thinking?"

"Being squashed together like that, like sardines in a tin, was unpleasant, dehumanizing, almost. For the first time I was able to appreciate what it must have been like to have been a slave, deprived of all rights, but even more so, deprived of all dignity. I'm glad we don't live in times like that."

"But some still do, you know. Poverty isn't all that different from slavery," he said.

I hadn't thought of that.

"Are you poor?" I asked.

I really am wicked. I shouldn't have asked a question like that. But he didn't seem to take offense—on the contrary. Rather, I sensed a hint of pride in his answer.

He nodded his head.

"My parents died recently," he said, "both of them, within a few months. I don't have any other family in Accra. My sister was sent back to our village, to an uncle we had never met. I think she must be very unhappy there. As for me, I was lucky. The Imam in our mosque made an announcement and a kind lady offered to adopt me. If it weren't for her I wouldn't be here today."

Mr. Mainoo interrupted our conversation. "OK, let's all move out into the courtyard now. I hope you've all benefited from this experience and that you won't forget it."

"Osman," I said, "I like you. Can we keep in touch? Do you have a mobile phone?"

Another stupid question. He didn't have a mobile phone. He said he did have an e-mail address but he had forgotten it.

Mr. Mainoo invited questions. There was an awkward silence. Then I put up my hand.

"Mr. Mainoo, sir," I said, "you told us that the British made the slave trade illegal in 1807."

"Correct," he said.

"What did they do with this dungeon, then?" I asked.

"They opened it for school tours," said the same wag as before. I recognized his voice. Fortunately for him Mr. Mainoo didn't hear his joke.

"The British government shut down the African Company of Merchants in 1821 and made the Gold Coast a British Crown Colony. They appointed Sir Charles McCarthy as governor. He sealed the dungeon and turned it into a water storage cistern. It wasn't opened again until modern times. Does that answer your question?"

My mind was racing. Sarah Bowdich and her husband left Cape Coast in 1818. So while Sarah was living in the Castle, the dungeon must still have been open. Miss Mensah caught my eye. She must have been reading my mind.

"Mr. Mainoo, sir," I said, "do you know the name Bowdich?"

"Yes, of course," he said, "The author of *Mission from Cape Coast to Ashantee*. Is that the man you mean? What about him?"

Miss Mensah told me later that Mr. Mainoo has a history degree from Legon.

"Actually," I said, "I was thinking about his wife."

"His wife?" Mr. Mainoo replied. "I didn't know he had a wife. Did he bring her to Cape Coast? None of the British brought their wives; at least, none that I know of."

The others were fidgeting. I suppose they were thirsty and looking forward to having a Coke.

"Mrs. Bowdich was here," I said. "I suppose she lived up there."

I pointed to the Governor's apartments which we had visited earlier.

"I just wondered whether they ever visited the dungeons; the Bowdich's, I mean," I said.

Mr. Mainoo shook his head, acknowledging defeat.

"I'm just your tour guide," he said. "I'm sorry, but I've no idea."

Miss Mensah took my hand and squeezed it.

"Good question," she said. "Now you'll have to read everything the two of them wrote, to see whether they ever mentioned it."

CHAPTER 9

Osman

One day, about half-way through the term, the headmaster came into Mr. Smith's class. We all stood up.

"Class," he said, "I have good news for you. Next Saturday we're going on our annual excursion. First we'll visit Cape Coast Castle and then we'll go on to the Kakum Forest. The bus will leave the school at 7 a.m. prompt. You can tell your parents that we expect to return by 5 p.m., but because of the traffic we might be late."

I was at the school at six, just as the sun was coming up. I wanted to make sure of a good seat. Mama's advice was to sit on the left to get the best view of the sea. I had my school bag with some fruit and snacks and a bottle of water in it.

I got my window seat, on the left in the third row and waited for the bus to fill up. At last only the seat next to me was still unoccupied. A boy called Mohammed entered the bus, panting and sweating, as if he had been running. He was one of the seniors in our class, which means he was a dunce.

"Late, as usual, Mohammed," said Mr. Kojo Smith who was sitting just behind the driver.

"Mo, Mo, Mo," his mates welcomed him.

"Ah, Mister Krakye," he greeted me.

"My name is Osman," I replied, but he didn't seem to hear.

We had hardly exchanged a word before that day. The seniors stuck to themselves.

"Have you been to Cape Coast before?" I asked him.

He laughed.

"Many times. Many, many times," he said. "Don't you know? In my holidays I work for my uncle as a mate. He drives a tro-tro from Accra to Takoradi and back. Sometimes two trips a day. He's teaching me to drive. I know this road like the back of my hand. What about you?"

I was ashamed. I shouldn't have asked him that question. I was fifteen and this was my first trip out of Accra. Ever. I didn't want to make a fool of myself by admitting that.

"What about me what?"

"Heh, I thought you were a *krakye*," he said. "I ask you a simple question and you answer 'what about me what?'"

But I had succeeded in diverting his attention.

"Listen," he said, "I've been thinking. You seem to be getting top marks in all our class tests, even though you started late. I wish I knew how you do it. As for me, this is my last chance. If I don't pass the next exams, I'll have to leave without a certificate. My father says he won't pay any more school fees for me. And I can't save anything from the chop money my uncle gives me."

The bus was on Ring Road now. Mohammed had taken it upon himself to be my guide, interrupting the thread of our conversation to point out landmarks.

"Kwame Nkrumah Circle, named after our first president."

Then, "Obetsebi Lamptey Circle, named after my uncle."

"Obetsebi Lamptey was your uncle?" I asked.

"Sort of," he said. "My surname is also Lamptey. I'm a Ga, like him. So I reckon he must have been my uncle."

"By the way," I asked him, "who was Obetsebi Lamptey?"

He didn't know. Neither did I.

"Mr. Smith, sir," Mohammed called, "who was Obetsebi Lamptey?"

"Never mind," said Mr. Smith, "he's not in the syllabus."

When we passed Kaneshie Market, Mohammed said, "How

about you giving me some extra lessons? I won't be able to pay you right away, but once I get my certificate, my uncle says he'll start giving me a regular wage and I won't forget you then."

What could I say? As it happened, I had brought a notebook with me. We decided to start there and then. Arithmetic first. Chaley, was he dumb. There was no way he was going to pass the exam.

"You should pray for a miracle," I told him.

He laughed. For Mohammed, life was a joke.

"Are you an observant Muslim?" I asked Mohammed.

"Of course," he said.

I had my doubts. He had been telling me about some of the adventures he had had with girls when he had had to sleep overnight in Takoradi. Not Muslim girls, of course.

And so the trip went. Places whose names I knew only from geography books, or not at all. McCarthy Hill, Panbros Salt Works, Weija Dam and Waterworks, Winneba Junction, Mankessim Junction. Then, up front, on the left, there was a castle. I knew it was a castle. I'd seen pictures of castles in books. I was quite excited.

"Is that Cape Coast Castle?" I asked Mohammed.

He laughed.

"No, we haven't reached Cape Coast yet."

"What is it then?"

He didn't know.

"Mr. Smith, sir, what's the name of that castle?" Mohammed asked.

He guessed what Mr. Smith's reply would be. Mr. Smith didn't seem to be aware that Mohammed was pulling his leg.

Mr. Smith said, "I don't know and it doesn't matter."

The senior boys echoed him as he continued, "It's not in the syllabus."

"Anomabu," Mohammed informed me as we entered the next village, seeking perhaps to redeem himself after having exposed his ignorance about the name of that castle on the hill.

He needn't have worried. I had read the sign, "Welcome to

Anomabu."

The rusty red iron roofs cascaded down to the sea. There were canoes on the beach and more on the sea.

"Anomabu," Mohammed repeated. "Bird's nest. *Anoma*–bird. *Ebuw*–nest. Anomabu–bird's nest. If you want to win the heart of a Fanti girl, just tell her, '*Wo ho ye fe se anomaa,*' you are as beautiful as a bird."

Mohammed's mind was full of girls. As far as he was concerned our Islamic rules don't apply to girls who aren't Muslims.

Our bus pulled up outside Cape Coast Castle. Mr. Kojo Smith marshaled us, two abreast, and led us inside. I was still with Mohammed. He might have joined one of his friends amongst the seniors but I guess he saw me now as the private magician who was going to conjure up his school leaving certificate. So he had to treat me as a friend.

In the lobby, Mr. Kojo Smith introduced our guide for the day: one Mr. Isaac Mainoo. Mr. Mainoo had a conversation on his mobile phone and told us that we would be joined shortly by a party from another school. To fill in the time we went to the Castle museum to watch a movie about the slave trade.

Back in the lobby we waited for the other school. They arrived within minutes: girls! I turned to Mohammed. Both his eyes and his mouth were wide open.

"Birds, Osman, my young brother," he said. "A whole flock of beautiful birds. And not a head scarf amongst them. Wow! Get out your catapult and take aim."

The girls were in their school uniforms: short black skirts and tight white shirts. I tried to control my bad thoughts. Their teacher wore slacks and a blouse. Her head scarf might have identified her as a Muslim but her slacks suggested otherwise. As she went to join the two men, Mohammed let out a loud whistle. Mr. Smith turned with an angry look but he couldn't spot the offender. And even if he had identified Mohammed, what could he have done? He was embarrassed. He turned to the lady, shaking his head and apologizing. She just smiled her forgiveness.

Mr. Mainoo addressed us.

"Ladies and gentlemen," he started.

Mohammed turned his head towards his mates.

"Yeah, yeah," he said.

Everyone laughed, even Mr. Mainoo and the girls' teacher; everyone except Mr. Kojo Smith, who scowled.

Mr. Mainoo smiled. He even made a joke about developing a loving relationship between our two schools. Then he told us that the Slave Trade was a serious matter and asked us to restrain what he called our youthful exuberance, while he led us through the Castle. He warned us that he was going to subject us to a painful mind-bending experience in the dungeons.

"That experience," he said, "may help you to understand the suffering of the slaves. If any of you have a weak heart or suffer from claustrophobia, now is the time for you to opt out."

"Mister Osman Book-long," Mohammed whispered, "what's that claustro stuff?"

"Claustrophobia. Fear of being shut up with no chance of escape," I told him.

We all trooped down into the dungeons. No one opted out. The first dungeon was quite small and it was nasty. After more than two hundred years the smell of slave bodies lingered on. There must have been about fifty of us, mixed up now, boys and girls. I had lost sight of Mohammed. Mr. Mainoo's voice echoed in the confined space. I no longer remember what he said, only that I felt like throwing up. We listened to him in silence. Not even Mohammed had anything to say. Then the experience started. Two men used a rope to herd us into a corner, shouting, "Move, move." Then the light went out and we were left in total darkness.

"Silence, please," said Mr. Mainoo's voice. "Try to focus your thoughts on those who were forced to pass months crowded in this fetid prison more than two centuries ago. Summon up their spirits. Concentrate. Now, please observe total silence until the light is switched on again."

There we were, crushed together, male and female. Mr. Mainoo had warned us boys not to let our hands wander.

He needn't have worried. My arms were pinned to my sides by bodies to my left and right and front and back. Then the Devil started his mischief. The thigh of the body in front of me pressed into my groin. The sweet smell of perfume entered my nostrils. Ripples of slight movement passed through the crowd as we tried to adjust to the discomfort. The rubbing caused an onrush of feelings I couldn't control. I struggled. I said a prayer. What a disgrace! What would the person think of me? I felt deeply ashamed. The thigh moved sideways, trying to create a space between us, perhaps, but that only made things worse. I dreaded what I would see when the light was switched on. All this time I had no time to think of the slaves of bygone days.

Mr. Mainoo spoke at last, telling us that as soon as the light went on we should join hands with our nearest neighbors and speak to them.

"For too long," he said, "our response to this sad history of ours has been silence and embarrassment. The time has come for us to begin to talk to one another about these things, and to begin to listen to the pain in the voices of our sisters and brothers in the diaspora, the descendants of those who passed through this place of terror long ago."

A hand found mine. It came from the direction of the perfume and the thigh. Then the light went on and there was such a noise. We were allowed to move apart. I wanted to escape but the girl held my hand. For a moment she looked into my eyes. Such eyes she had! I still remember that first look as I write this. Then she dropped her gaze and my shame returned. But when she raised her eyes again there was no enmity in them. Rather, she smiled.

"My name is Akosua Annan," she said.

I told her my name and the name of my school. At once I realized how stupid that was. Our school's name was written in bold letters on the green tee-shirts we were all wearing.

Then we talked. She asked if I was a Muslim. I told her proudly that I was and asked her if she was a Christian. That seemed to confuse her. She said that she was a free-thinker.

I asked her what that was, but she quickly changed the subject and reminded me that Mr. Mainoo had asked us to discuss our reaction to the crowding and darkness and silence.

"Osman, what was going on in your mind during that long two minutes?" she asked.

The Devil was really busy that day. I wondered whether that Miss Akosua Annan was trying to embarrass me. Of course she must have guessed what had been in my mind, and of course I couldn't tell her the truth, so I repeated something that I'd read in a library book. I told her that most of the slaves were captured in the North and that living in poverty was not all that different from living in slavery. That is what I said.

There was a silence between us and then she asked me, "Don't you want to know what I was thinking?"

That was the last thing I wanted to hear from her, but it would have been rude not to reply.

"What?" I asked.

She said, "I felt so uncomfortable with all of us squashed up like sardines. For the first time I understood what it might have been like to be enslaved and imprisoned in that smelly dungeon."

I asked her if she knew what it was like to be poor.

Then she asked me, "Are you poor?"

Well, I used to be poor until my parents died. Now, thanks to Mama Zainab, I'm better off. But I didn't tell her that. I told her that I was an orphan and I told her about Afia being sent to the North. Afterwards I was sorry about that. It was as if I were trying to punish her for something which wasn't her fault. Then, as Mr. Mainoo called us to follow him, she said some words I haven't forgotten.

She said, "Osman, I like you. Can we keep in touch?"

No one had ever said anything like that to me before, certainly no girl. And then we were separated.

Mohammed said, "Heh, Krakye Osman, how did you do it? You caught the prettiest bird in that whole bunch."

I caught her and then I let her go.

CHAPTER 10

Akosua

Ama Osei, dearly beloved Ama Osei. Seriously overweight. Often overburdened with problems: her obesity, her performance in exams, her relationship with her parents, who always seemed to be on the point of divorce, money problems. Dearly beloved Ama Osei, kind and generous to a fault. One couldn't ask for a better friend: loyal, concerned, supportive, affectionate.

On the first day of term, Ama was absent. She was one of the few day-girls. Ama would have loved to be one of us boarders but her father said he couldn't afford the fees. So she stayed at home with her ever-bickering parents and took a *tro-tro* to school every morning.

Even in a sleepy town like Cape Coast traveling by *tro-tro* is not easy, especially during the rush hours. Ghanaians don't like standing in queues. As the *tro-tro* comes to a stop and the door opens there's a scramble to get in. First come, first served. Survival of the fittest.

"It's the only time my weight comes in useful," Ama would say.

Ama had to get up at five to make sure she wasn't late for school. She would often arrive just as the bell rang, sweating and anxious. Not a good way to start the day.

When she was absent the first day, we guessed she had had trouble with transport and would turn up in due course. When she didn't, I thought to call her on her mobile phone. But we have to hand in our mobile phones, so mine was locked up with all the others in the headmistress's store.

"Don't worry," said Geraldine, "maybe she has a cold or a touch of malaria. She'll be here tomorrow."

But she wasn't.

Our first class was maths with Miss Jones.

"Please Miss," Geraldine told her, "Ama Osei hasn't come back to school this term."

Miss Jones said she'd tell the headmistress.

On day three we had our first class with Miss Mensah. We expressed our concern to her, Geraldine and I.

"Does anyone remember Ama Osei's mobile phone number?" she asked, but no one did.

"Akosua Annan," said Miss Mensah, "come with me."

She gave the class some work to do and we went to see the headmistress.

"Ama Osei?" said the headmistress. "Oh yes, Miss Jones reported her absence to me. I tried to get through to her parents' home but there was no connection."

"Akosua says she has Ama's number on her mobile phone," Miss Mensah said.

I caught a glimpse of the inside of the headmistress's store: rows and rows of mobile phones, each with a yellow sticker bearing the name of its owner.

I called Ama's number. Recorded message: "The number you have dialed is either switched off or out of coverage area …"

They had a conference. Neither of them knew where Ama's home was. I did. So it was decided that Miss Mensah would drive into town at break, with me as her guide.

Mr. and Mrs. Osei and their family live in an upstairs apartment in an old building at the lower end of Jukwa Road, near the Town Hall. Not the classiest part of town, but at least it has a good sea breeze. We climbed the outside staircase. Miss

Mensah knocked on the door and called out, "*Agoo!*" through the open Naco louvers. No answer. She knocked again. Abena came to the window. Abena is the ten-year old illiterate girl from Mrs. Osei's village who works for them as a child-minder and general dogsbody. She was carrying Ama's little sister on her back. Abena knows me but she didn't open the front door. I guess it was locked, that she'd been left locked in with the child. I spoke through the window.

"Abena," I told her in Fanti, "this is our teacher, Miss Mensah. We've come to find out why Ama hasn't come to school."

Abena was close to tears.

"They took her to hospital," was all she said. She used the English word "hospital."

"Hospital? What's wrong with her?" I asked, but Abena just shook her head.

"Ask her which hospital," said Miss Mensah, but Abena had no idea.

Cape Coast Hospital is just a kilometer down Beulah Road across the Fosu Lagoon. We were there in half a jiffy. Miss Mensah pushed in at the head of the queue of out-patients waiting to speak to the guy at the reception desk.

"Sorry," she said. "Just a quick question."

In Ghana, if you wait your turn, you'll never get anything done.

"I hate doing that," she said, "but this is an emergency."

We found our way to the gynae ward. It wasn't difficult; it's not a big hospital and there were sign boards. The benches in the waiting room were full. I saw Mrs. Osei. She was asleep, her mouth sagging.

"Miss," I said, "Ama's mother. Shall I wake her?"

"No," said Miss Mensah. "She looks exhausted. Let's see if we can find the Ward Sister."

She sent me out of hearing distance while she talked to the Sister. I watched them. Miss Mensah asked questions. She had a serious expression on her face. Then she beckoned.

"Sister Ababio," she said, "this is Akosua Annan. She's one of Ama's school friends."

Then she turned to me.

"It's not visiting time," she said, "but Sister has agreed to let us go and see Ama for just a few minutes."

Ama was in a ward with five other patients. She was on a drip and there was a tube in her nose. She was fast asleep. She looked terrible, her face all gray. We stood there for a moment, but there was no point in waiting.

"Thank you, Sister," said Miss Mensah. "We'll come back at visiting time."

Mrs. Osei was still sleeping as we left.

Miss Mensah hardly said a word during the drive back to school. She almost hit a car coming out of a junction near Kotokoraba Market.

"Sorry," she said, "my fault. I was deep in thought."

That made two of us, deep in thought.

She parked the car and I started to open the door.

"Akos, wait," she said.

"Have you guessed what is wrong with Ama?"

I had guessed, but I didn't want to risk getting it wrong.

"She's had an abortion, a botched backstreet abortion. She's lost a lot of blood. I've told you because you've seen her. I think it would be better if you didn't say anything about it. Can you invent a lie to tell your classmates? Promise?"

I promised and she went to report to the headmistress. I told Geraldine and the others that Ama was in hospital but that she was sleeping and we weren't allowed to see her. I said I didn't know what was wrong with her. I found it difficult to concentrate.

That afternoon we went to see her again: the headmistress and Miss Mensah, with Geraldine, Lily and me representing our class. The ward was full of visitors. Mr. and Mrs. Osei were sitting by Ama's bed. They got up and shook hands with the headmistress and Miss Mensah, and nodded to us. Mr. Osei offered the headmistress his chair but she declined. Ama looked much the same as when we saw her earlier in the day. She was awake but most of the time kept her eyes closed. It was all rather awkward. Our headmistress made a little speech, telling Ama's parents how sorry we all were and asking if there was anything we could do. I went to the side of Ama's bed opposite the drip and took her hand. She looked at me but I found it difficult to tell what her look meant. Eventually the headmistress, as is our custom, asked for permission to leave. Mr. and Mrs. Osei rose to see us off. I was about to join them but Ama squeezed my hand.

"Akos, thank you for coming," she whispered, her voice hoarse. "Tell Miss Mensah she was right. I was so stupid, deceived by sweet words. He hasn't even had the courage to come and visit me."

I took a tissue from the bedside table and wiped the tears from her eyes.

"Who was it?" I asked, but she just shook her head, released my hand and turned on her side, with her back to me. I hesitated, unsure what to do next. Then Geraldine was at the door beckoning to me.

Next morning, halfway through Miss Jones's maths, the headmistress came into our classroom with Miss Mensah. They both had long faces. Miss Jones stood aside.

"Girls," said the headmistress, "I have sad news for you; sad, sad news."

She paused, took out a tissue and wiped her eyes.

"Your classmate Ama Osei died early this morning."

For a moment she seemed about to break down. Then she pulled herself together.

"This will come as a terrible shock to the whole school, but particularly to you, her classmates. I don't know what else to say.

"All your lessons are suspended for the rest of the day. I have asked the psychiatrist at Cape Coast Hospital to come and talk to you. He should be here any time now. I've also asked the chaplains from our sister and brother schools in the town to come and offer individual counseling to any of you who feel the need for it. In the meantime, Miss Mensah and Miss Jones will stay with you. Now, are there any questions?"

Lily Mends was the only one who put up her hand.

"Please Miss," she said, "may we all attend the funeral?"

These days Christians in Ghana often have the bodies of their dead relatives embalmed and then they leave them in the mortuary for weeks, sometimes months, while they organize the funeral. But this doesn't apply to those who die suddenly from accidents or suicide or unmentionable diseases. Ama's funeral took place just four days after she died. At her parents' request it was a low-key affair: no specially printed brochures, no tee-shirts bearing her image and only two tributes. Our class represented the whole school, wearing our school uniforms. Generally, the lid of the coffin is removed in the church to allow the mourners to file past and bid a last farewell to the deceased. They left Ama's lid screwed firmly down.

In the single tribute from the family one of Ama's uncles recited the short story of her life and managed to say precisely nothing about the girl we all knew.

I had been given the job of delivering a tribute on behalf of our class and the school. I'd typed it out and discussed it with Miss Mensah. It was only a little less bland than the uncle's. I was called to the front of the church. I put my script on the lectern but when I opened my mouth to read from it, I disgraced myself: I broke down in tears. There was a big lump in my throat and I couldn't say a word. Miss Mensah came forward and gave me a tissue.

"Shall I read it for you?" she asked.

I shook my head and my voice came back.

"Thank you," I said. "I'll manage."

I forgot all about my script.

"Ama's last words to me," I said, "were, 'I was so stupid, deceived by sweet words,' and 'He hasn't even had the courage to come and visit me.' I asked her who 'he' was. She didn't tell me.

"I wonder if that 'he' is in this church today. Man or boy? I have no idea. But whichever he is, he is guilty of murder. He deceived Ama with his sweet words. He used her to satisfy his lust. He made her pregnant and then he didn't have the guts to face up to the consequences. He took her to a backstreet abortionist and together they murdered her; they murdered our kind, gentle, loving friend, Ama Osei. I have been given the task of speaking for my classmates and for our school. We loved Ama. Her death has been a traumatic experience for us. It has confronted all of us, young as we are, with the harsh reality of our own mortality. We share Mr. and Mrs. Osei's grief and that of their other children."

Then I ran my eyes over the congregation and challenged the murderers to stand up and identify themselves. Of course, no one did.

"Ama, rest in peace," I said. "You will always be in our thoughts."

I stepped down. Then someone, it might have been Geraldine, began to clap. That is not good manners in church, especially during a funeral service, but our class joined in, then the rest of the congregation, and finally they all stood up and continued to clap. Back in my seat, I collapsed in tears again.

The Minister thanked me for a moving oration. He told the bereaved parents that they should have faith and be comforted because God knew the reason for Ama's death. He urged all present to live lives free of sin, because no one can predict when they will die.

On Sunday, the *Mirror* carried a picture of Ama on the front page and the headline, in big black letters, "CAPE COAST SCHOOLGIRL DIES." The subheading read, "VICTIM OF BACKSTREETS ABORTION."

CHAPTER 11

Osman

Iwas at my desk, studying geometry, when Mama called.

She had taken two *Gye Nyame* plastic chairs out onto the sidewalk, in front of the shop. By her side sat a police officer, a large woman, in uniform.

"Hallo Osman," she said, "do you remember me?" and then she greeted me again, this time in Hausa.

Her presence disturbed me. I hadn't seen her since she had taken Afia away.

Mama said, "Osman, bring another chair."

"Sit," she said.

She had a serious expression on her face.

"Osman, I'm sure you will remember that, after your mother died, it was Sergeant Fianko who took your sister to your uncle in the North. Now your uncle has sent her a letter. I think you should read it, but be prepared for a shock."

She handed me the letter. It had a printed heading, "Abdul Alhassan, Licensed Letter Writer, P. O. Box 17, Saboba," and was addressed to "Sergeant Mabel Fianko, Police Training Depot, Nsawam Road, Accra."

It read, "Dear Sergeant Fianko, This is Boyan Nabu, brother of the late Sergeant Onafor Said. Last year, after the death of my brother and his wife, you brought their daughter Afia to me to look after her. I regret to inform you that Afia has been taken ill. When she started coughing blood, I took her from our village to the Saboba Medical Centre, where she is on admission. My wife is staying with her there. She is crying most of the time and calling for her brother Osman. I should be most grateful if you would find Osman and tell him that his sister is calling for him."

Underneath was typed, "The mark of Boyan Nabu" and an inked cross, and underneath that, a declaration from Mr. Alhassan that he had translated the contents of the letter into the vernacular and read it back to the said Boyan Nabu, who had confirmed that that is what he intended to say.

I didn't know what to think. I had forgotten my sister Afia, put her out of my mind as I concentrated on making a success of my new life. Now she was sick. Coughing blood. That sounded serious. But what could I do? How could I go to see her? I was overwhelmed with a sense of guilt and foreboding.

I looked up. Both of them were watching me.

Mama said, "Osman, Christmas is coming. I'm going to lock up the store for ten days over the holidays. Amadu will drive us to Saboba. If Afia is well enough and if your uncle agrees, we'll bring her back to Accra. Now, what do you say to that?"

What could I say? I was so happy. I knelt before her and whispered, "Thank you, Mama."

"Don't be silly," she said. "I've never been to the North and I think I deserve a holiday. And, Osman, don't worry about Afia. I'm sure she'll be better by the time we arrive. And if she isn't, she'll get better as soon as she sees you. Now, go to your study. First, look for Saboba on your big map of Ghana. You'll find it right on the Togo border, east of Tamale.

"Then write two letters, one to your uncle and one to Afia. Tell them to expect us about the 26th of December. My old Bluebird will need three days to get to Saboba."

She said I should address the envelopes care of the Letter Writer, Mr. Alhassan.

Mama sent the Bluebird to the workshop for a thorough overhaul. She bought a new set of tires. Master Zarifou advised her which essential spare parts we should take: fan belts, light bulbs, fuses; and also a set of spanners and screw drivers. Mama appointed me honorary chief mechanic. We stowed plastic gallons with petrol and water, brake fluid and engine oil in the boot.

Mama shopped for presents, food and soap and *obroni wawu* clothes to take to Afia and my uncle's family, a family I had never seen but which Mama seemed about to adopt as her own.

We set off early on Christmas Eve which was a Saturday. That night we slept in Kumasi at the house of Mama's sister, my new aunt by adoption whom I hadn't met before. Auntie Esi is a Roman Catholic so she invited us to go to Midnight Mass at St Peter's Cathedral with her. I told Mama that I didn't want to go, that it was forbidden for Muslims to go to church. Mama said not to be silly; and I had no choice. In the end I was glad I went. Some things in church seemed very different from our Friday prayers but some were not so different. The main difference was that, whereas in the mosque men and women pray separately, in the church they are all mixed up. In the mosque we are taught to be silent whereas in the church they sing hymns. The Christians also kneel, though not as we do. They also have a sermon and a collection; and at the end of the service, they also greet one another in peace. What still puzzles me is whether their God and our Allah are the same.

Auntie Esi wanted us to stay for Christmas but Mama said we had important business in Saboba. We left Kumasi quite late on Christmas Day so we didn't get to Tamale until after dark.

Mama said, "I don't have a sister in Tamale, so we'll have to look for a hotel."

Because it was a holiday most of the hotels were full but we found one at last. Mama took one room and I shared another with Amadu. That was the first time I had stayed in a hotel. It wasn't a fancy hotel. The bathroom was down the corridor and I had to bath out of a bucket.

The road from Tamale to Yendi was not bad but the last 50 kilometers to Saboba was full of potholes. Mama kept telling Amadu not to drive so fast. Also, the air was full of dust from the Harmattan, so visibility was poor. And it was hot! I've never experienced such heat. I don't know how people can live in that climate. But we survived without a breakdown and without an accident. The first thing we did when we reached Saboba was to spread our prayer mats by the side of the road and give thanks to Allah for our safe arrival.

I had looked Saboba up on the Internet. It's a small town with only one telephone and a population of less than four thousand. Sergeant Fianko had told us to look for the Letter Writer in front of the Post Office. We found him there, sitting on a chair in the shade of a mango tree. His painted signboard was nailed to the tree trunk. It read "Abdul Alhassan, Licensed Letter Writer and Commissioner of Oaths," with his address. On a small folding table in front of him there was an old-fashioned typewriter like the one I had seen my father use. Mr. Alhassan was hammering away at the keys. A customer sat on a bench in front of him. Mr. Alhassan paused to ask the man a question. Then he saw us. He rose to his feet.

"Good afternoon, Madame," he said, "Can I help you?"

He spoke to his customer and the man got up and pulled the bench back so we could sit.

Mama greeted him. "Mr. Alhassan, good afternoon. We know you by name, but you don't know us. Osman, show the letter to Mr. Alhassan."

He put on an ancient pair of spectacles and read the letter. Then he read it again and nodded wisely.

"So you are Osman, Afia's brother," he said.

"Yes sir," I said. "When Sergeant Fianko gave me my uncle's letter, I replied and also wrote to my sister. I sent the letters care of you, sir, and asked you to deliver them to Afia and my uncle. I said we would be here on 26th December."

Mr. Alhassan shook his head.

"I didn't receive your letter. When did you post it?"

"Two weeks ago."

He shook his head again.

"Letters from Accra take a long time to reach us. Sometimes they don't arrive at all. Madame. Excuse me, who are you?"

"I'm sorry. I should have introduced myself. My name is Hajia Zainab. I adopted Osman when his mother died. Mr. Alhassan, please tell us. Where can we find Afia and Osman's uncle?"

Mr. Alhassan wasn't sure but suggested that we inquire at the Medical Centre. Mama thanked him and offered to pay him for his help but he held up his hands and shook his head.

At the hospital the nurse in charge told us that Afia was still there but that she was being kept in the isolation ward and we would have to see Dr. Edith for permission to see her. The doctor would be back on duty at four, when it was a little cooler. So we went to the Rest House and booked two rooms. We had something to eat and drink and then we went to our rooms. I switched on the overhead fan and had a nap.

When we got back to the Medical Centre, Dr. Edith agreed to see us. She was a white American lady. Mama did the talking, telling her that after my mother's death she had adopted me but that Afia had been sent to my father's village to be adopted by my uncle.

"Afia has tuberculosis," said the doctor. "I'm afraid the outlook is not good. She had been coughing for a long time, especially in the morning. In the afternoon she would have fever and at night she would sweat so much that it disturbed her sleep. Then she began to lose weight and her skin began to lose color. But it was only when she became so weak that she couldn't work anymore and then began to cough blood, that your uncle brought her to us. We have very limited laboratory facilities here and we don't have X-ray equipment, but the symptoms suggested strongly that she had tuberculosis and that the disease was already at an advanced stage. Fortunately we had stocks of suitable antibiotics. After the first two weeks of treatment the disease should no longer be contagious, but we can't be sure, so we've kept her in isolation.

Only our staff and her uncle's second wife are allowed to go near her. She and her aunt have only a few words of Hausa in common. She is miserable and lonely and she has been crying for Osman. It is good that you have come."

Dr. Edith gave each of us a face mask and put one on herself. Then we went to see Afia. She was in a bed behind a screen. There was a woman I didn't recognize sitting on a mat nearby. Both of them wore face masks. When Afia recognized me she was so excited that she tried to sit up. The effort was too much for her. Dr. Edith propped her up on pillows and sent a nurse to bring us some chairs. I held Afia's hands.

I said, "My little sister, I have come at last."

Behind the white mask, her face was a shock. While her complexion used to be dark, now she looked so pale. She was thin, smaller than when I last saw her in Accra. And yet she was more than a year older.

She spoke in Hausa. Her voice was hoarse.

"Osman, I am so glad to see you. I have missed you so much. I have been so lonely here."

The nurse brought another pillow. The strange woman spoke to Dr. Edith in a language I didn't understand.

Dr. Edith asked me, "Osman, do you understand Lekpokpam, your father's language? No? Well, this is your uncle's younger wife. She has been so good, staying with Afia all the time she has been here. The trouble is that Afia still speaks only a few words of Lekpokpam and your aunt speaks only a few words of Hausa. Now greet your aunt and I'll explain to her who you are and who Hajia Zainab is."

My aunt bent her knees and smiled weakly. There was no shaking of hands.

After only a few minutes Dr. Edith said, "I think you must go now. Afia tires quickly. I am so glad you have come. You must come again early tomorrow morning, before it is too hot. I'll give her a sedative to make sure she has a good sleep. You can talk some more tomorrow morning."

When we got to the Medical Centre the next morning, Afia was dead.

CHAPTER 12

Akosua

While we were still trying to adjust ourselves to the harsh reality of Ama's death, our President announced a major reshuffle of her government. The Ministries of Education and Culture were merged. Shortly after her appointment the new Minister announced a National Festival of the Arts for Schools. There were several categories including short stories, poetry, drama, music and dance, painting and sculpture, and oratory. She instructed every secondary school to appoint a coordinator. Talent spotting would start within each school and then proceed through competitions at district and regional levels to a major festival at the National Theatre in Accra. At assembly our head-mistress announced that she had appointed Miss Mensah as our coordinator.

"To minimize the damage to your formal academic work," she said, "each of you will be allowed to sign up for no more than two categories."

I chose short stories and oratory.

For my short story I went back to Sarah Bowdich's *The Booroom Slave*, which was set partly in Cape Coast. Writing in 1828, Mrs. Bowdich told that story from her own point of view: that of a young English lady. Writing nearly two centuries later, this young Ghanaian lady decided to re-tell the story from the point of view of the enslaved girl, Inna. I called it *Inna's Tale*. Since this was fiction, I took some liberties, adding a visit to the dungeons of Cape Coast Castle to give Inna a chance to confront Sarah with the enormity of British responsibility for the slave trade and the hypocrisy of some of the leading supporters of abolition. I wrote with passion, sometimes even crying when I read what I had written. Miss Mensah was a great help, offering positive and sensitive criticism of my various drafts. I'm sure she helped all the other entrants in the same way. After all, she was our English teacher.

Later, she invited the heads of the English departments at three other schools to act as independent judges of our entries. To my great elation, my story came out top and was sent on for judging at the district level. Now, there are plenty of top secondary schools in Cape Coast, some much older and bigger than ours, including Wesley Girls and Holy Child for girls; Mfantsipim, Adisadel and St. Augustine's for boys; and Ghana National and Aggrey Zion for both. The competition must have been tough. This time the judges were three professors of English at the University of Cape Coast. They judged blind. That means that we the authors were given numbers and the judges didn't know our names. Again, I was lucky enough to succeed. Wow!

After that the Region was a piece of cake. None of the other districts in the Central Region are a patch on Cape Coast Metro when it comes to education. So my piece, *Inna's Tale,* went on to represent the Central Region in the national competition. This time, the judges were distinguished published authors appointed by the Ghana Association of Writers.

I put my heart and soul into writing that story, but once I completed the final version, there was nothing more to do but dream.

With oratory, a grand name for debating, it was different. Our three-member team, with me in the lead and Geraldine and Lily in support, had to argue and charm (and sometimes even cheat) our way through countless debates at school, district, regional and national levels. The ultimate prize for the winning team was to represent Ghana at the African Schools Debating Championship and perhaps, perhaps at the World School Debating Championship.

For the prepared debates, my job was to establish the factual basis for our case. The Internet usually took the sweat out of that.

Geraldine was the critic. Hers was to ferret out errors of fact or logic in my draft, in preparation for the onslaught of our opposition.

Lily's task was to identify opportunities for emotion, particularly humor.

Along the way we learned some dirty tricks: it always helps to make your opposition look stupid, or dishonest, or unethical, particularly on issues of human rights, gender or the environment. All this has nothing to do with the rightness or the wrongness of the arguments on either side: your job is to persuade the judges of your skill in making your case, even if, privately, you don't believe a word of it.

That kept us busy. We had two debates a month. Once we had overcome our nervousness and persuaded ourselves that we were a winning team, it was great fun. Best of all was to visit the boys' schools and beat them on their own ground! And for me, in the final stages there was a totally unexpected benefit, a complete surprise. But more of that later.

The girls in our school come from all over the country, from the Upper East and the Upper West, from Nzima in the south-west and from the Volta Region in the east. That makes it difficult to organize meetings of the Parent-Teacher Association. They usually have just one meeting a year, at the beginning of the third term, which is also when we have our annual speech day. Even then many of the parents find it difficult to take time off their work and I guess they might also have a problem with the cost of traveling to Cape Coast and staying in a hotel. So the meetings are generally not well attended. Of course, since I'm neither a parent nor a teacher you won't find me there either. So this story is second-hand, as told to me by my dear mother, with some additions from my father.

In the course of her report our headmistress mentioned the tragic death of Ama Osei. By that time there had been an inquest and the coroner's verdict was that Ama had died as a result of "complications arising from an illegal abortion procured by a person or persons as yet unknown." Police investigations had failed to uncover the identity of those unknown persons.

When the chairperson invited questions or comments, Charity Baah's mother, who had come from Accra, stood up and introduced herself. She said how shocked she and her husband had been by the circumstances of the death of her daughter Charity's classmate. She urged the police (who were not present) to continue their investigations. Then she dropped a bombshell.

"My husband and I," she said, "have heard disturbing reports concerning goings-on in the late Ama's class. According to these reports, school periods which should properly have been devoted to the syllabus and getting our daughters through their exams, have been used for other purposes. One teacher's name in particular has been mentioned.

"I understand that some of these sessions dealt with issues such as politics and sex and that the legalization of crimes such as abortion and prostitution was proposed. I have discussed the matter with the headmistress and she has confirmed to me that this improper use of school time was made without her authority and indeed without her knowledge.

"I should now like to propose a motion, as follows:

"This meeting of the Parent Teacher Association strongly urges that the school authorities and, if need be, the Ministry of Education, should carry out a thorough investigation into reports of the use of school time for undesirable purposes. If the reports turn out to be correct, the teacher concerned should be suitably disciplined and, if appropriate, made to face the full severity of the law.

"May I have a seconder, please?"

"I second the motion," said Charity's father. "In doing so I should like to draw attention to the possibility that there might be a link between the issues raised in these illicit sessions and the subsequent behavior of the unfortunate Ama, which led to her premature demise."

My parents share my admiration for Miss Mensah. They had chatted to her before the meeting and encouraged her to keep up her good work. They were outraged by what they perceived as a witch-hunt.

My father said, "Madam chair, a point of order."

"Proceed, Professor Annan," said the chair.

"This motion doesn't appear on the agenda. It should be disallowed."

Madam chair rejected this, saying that she accepted the motion under "matters arising." A heated debate followed. The majority view was that the proposed investigation could do no harm. If the allegations were found to be without any basis, the matter would end there. If the conscience of the teacher concerned was clear, she should have no fear.

We know that the teachers at the school have mixed feelings about Miss Mensah. Some of them resent her popularity with the girls. Others feel she's just too big for her boots. We know this because conversations overheard in the school spread like a bush fire in the Harmattan.

One of the teachers demanded a secret ballot on the motion. I guess she didn't want to reveal her views.

Miss Jones, bless her, said, "This motion is a gross interference with our freedom to teach as best we know how. I shall vote against it."

Through all this Miss Mensah's face, my mother says, showed no emotion; but I guess that inside her she was seething.

The next time we met with her she gave us her version of what had transpired at the PTA meeting. The story was much the same as my parents' but Miss Mensah mentioned no names.

"You may recall," she said then, "that when we started our weekly discussions, I suggested that we should treat them as confidential. The suggestion was accepted without dissent.

"That undertaking of confidentiality has clearly been dishonored. I am not going to ask the culprit or culprits to own up. That would savor of a witch-hunt. I leave it to their consciences to handle the consequences of their breach of trust.

"The first of those consequences is that our discussions will cease forthwith. That is because I have been placed on suspension with immediate effect and until the committee of inquiry submits its report. So I've come to see you today, with the headmistress's permission, to say goodbye, at least for the present.

"I have considered submitting my resignation but since that might be seen by some as an admission of guilt I have decided against it. One last thing before I leave you. Because of the outrageous and slanderous allegation that there might have been a connection between our discussions and Ama Osei's death, I understand that some or all of you may be interviewed by police officers. I trust you will tell them the truth, all the truth, and nothing but the truth."

She had taken her bag from the table and was halfway to the door when I spoke up.

"Miss," I said.

She turned. I was close to tears. I stood up.

"Miss Mensah," I said, "I just want to say that you are the best teacher I have ever had. And I know that that goes for most of my classmates."

"Thank you, Akosua," she said. "And thank you all. You've been a great class and I hope we will meet again in better circumstances in the not too distant future."

Miss Mensah did not teach at our school again. The University of Ghana English Department offered her a lectureship and she tendered her resignation soon after the committee of inquiry submitted its report. The committee cleared her name completely and condemned the gossip-mongers.

Ama's murderers have not been discovered and probably never will be.

CHAPTER 13

Ghana Muntie

The Nation's Newspaper

Accra, Monday, March 6

DARK HORSES TRIUMPH IN DEBATING CONTEST

By Virginia Thompson, *Ghana Muntie*'s Literary, Art and Music Editor

On Saturday night at the National Theatre, a full house of exuberant young people and distinguished invited guests, including Her Excellency the President of the Republic of Ghana, witnessed the final debate in the National Schools Debating Competition. Both the winning team and the best speaker were surprise winners from little-known schools.

The debate was the climax of this year's National Festival of the Arts for Schools.

Music and dance are our national language. Throughout the past week the regional winners regaled us with brilliant performances of traditional drumming, palm wine guitar music, high life, hip hop and rap; and also a Mozart sonata for piano and violin and great singing by the winners of the National School Choirs Competition. We saw some superb demonstrations of dance, including not only *Adowa* and *Kete*, *Adzewa*, *Tokpe*, *Bamaya* and *Kpatsa* from our own rich heritage, but also ballet from the West and Bharata Natyam from India. On stage there were inspired and inspiring recitals of Anansesem and readings of poetry, in English as well as in Twi, Ga, Ewe, Dagaare and Hausa. For just a few cedis, visitors could take home a CD with a selection of the best music entries or a volume of the previously announced winning short stories and poems. In the foyer there was an exhibition of paintings, photographs, sculpture and original craft work, all by students.

This astonishing manifestation of talent is no more than the tip of the proverbial iceberg, representing only the young artists who made it through the district and regional stages to the finals. During the past twelve months, hundreds of teachers in high schools throughout the country have identified and nurtured the talents of their charges. What we saw and heard during the past week was a vibrant tribute to their dedication and hard work, as they encouraged the youngsters in their care to hone their creative skills. While only a selected few made it to Accra, all the participants, without exception, are entitled to derive a sense of pride and satisfaction from their participation, and some of those who didn't win this year will no doubt make it to the finals next year.

The successful completion of the National Festival of the Arts for Schools is also a tribute to the vision, imagination and trust of our Minister of Education and Culture whose brainchild it was and who has made it all possible.

Fine oratory is a skill which is highly valued in our culture, second only to music and dance, so it was fitting that the highlight of Saturday night's function was the final of the National Schools' Debating Competition.

The final pitted the Cape Coast Girls' High School against the Maamobi Boys' SHS, Central Region versus Greater Accra. Both teams had defeated rivals from better known schools on their way to the top.

(continued on page 88)

CHAPTER 14

The Debate

(continued from page 87)

The MC called for silence and the band played a fanfare. Two girls, dressed in their school uniforms of black skirts and white shirts, came on-stage from the left to the sound of deafening applause and high-pitched ululations from their supporters. Seconds later two boys followed from the right, dressed in black jeans and green tee shirts with the name of their school emblazoned on the chest. The MC introduced the contestants: Akosua Annan and Lily Mends for the Cape Coast Girls' School and Osman Said and Jackson Brew for Maamobi Boys'. They all shook hands. The MC explained the rules and called forward the team leaders, Akosua and Osman, to jointly choose one of six sealed envelopes. With a grand flourish he tore open the envelope they selected and read out the subject for the evening's debate: "The problem of poverty in Ghana is insoluble." The words came up on the screens on either side of the stage. At the toss of a coin, Akosua became the proposer and Osman the opposer of the motion.

"The teams will now retire to separate rooms for forty minutes," announced the MC. "When they return, Akosua and Osman will each have precisely seven minutes to argue their cases. After Lily and Jackson have had their say, the judges will select the winning team and the best speaker."

A digital stopwatch started ticking away the seconds on the screens.

The forty minutes passed quickly with a performance of works by Ephraim Amu sung by the winner of the National Schools' Choir Competition. Then the four speakers returned to the stage and took their seats. There was an excited buzz in the auditorium.

Akosua Annan stepped up to the lectern. The MC pressed a button and rang a bell and the seconds of Akosua's seven minutes started running on the screens: 0:01, 0:02, 0:03 …

Akosua looked out into the darkened auditorium.

"Poverty," she began, "is an abomination. It thwarts the mental and physical growth of children and it humiliates their parents. Few will dispute that. But that is not the subject of our debate. We are debating the proposition that the problem of poverty in Ghana is insoluble. I shall do my best to demonstrate the truth of that proposition."

"Four out of every ten Ghanaians live in poverty," she said. "Many children go to bed hungry most nights. 'Go to bed' is of course just an English expression. Many sleep on a floor mat, not in a bed.

"The poor lack access to clean drinking water, basic sanitary facilities, health services, quality education and electricity. The modern sector of our economy discriminates against them. Bank managers ride in shiny four-wheel-drive monsters; their rural customers are shod in *chaley wote.* Foreign loans and grants intended for poverty alleviation tend to evaporate as they trickle down to the intended beneficiaries."

"Our proverbs," she said, "offer evidence that poverty has dogged us throughout our history. The late Mrs. Peggy Appiah's book *Bu Me Bɛ* lists nearly a hundred proverbs concerning poverty. *Ohiani nni yɔnkoɔ,* 'poor man no friend,' is perhaps the best known example.

"Our first President, Osagyefo Dr. Kwame Nkrumah of blessed memory, launched a war on poverty. His favored weapon was education, which he believed would transform Ghanaian society. His government built many schools. My grandparents and my parents who are with us here tonight, and I suppose many others in our distinguished audience, were amongst the beneficiaries. Education did indeed help many to escape from poverty, but many others, too many, were left behind. In this respect, Nkrumah failed, and all the soldiers and civilians who succeeded him in office have failed, too. Poverty has been stubbornly persistent."

"Given that history," she asked, "can we have any confidence that our lady president, who has honored us with her presence here tonight, will do better? Much loved and admired and respected as she is, I think not. I fear not.

"It seems that the poor will always be with us. Diarrhea and dysentery, malaria and measles will continue to take our children from us. The parents of those children will continue to build their rude dwellings near watercourses only to see them washed away by the next heavy rains. But what choice do they have? They can't afford to buy land on higher ground. Poverty has trapped them.

"Our leaders of the past fifty years plus had their faults, no doubt, but they were not bad people and they were no fools. None of them lacked devotion and commitment to this country and its people. Surely, then, if there were a solution to the problem of poverty, they would have discovered it by now?

"Our farmers suffer years of drought. When the rains do come those same farmers' fields are submerged. I am reminded of the words of the English poet, Christopher Logue: 'When I flog salt, it rains; when I sell flour, it blows.' It seems the poor cannot win. *Ohiani nni yɔnkoɔ.*

"The Millennium Development Project—proclaimed to effect an end to worldwide poverty by 2015—is no more than politicians' talk. Does anyone really believe the promises that Ghana will become a middle income country in the near future?"

The screen showed the elapsed minutes and seconds: 5.58, 5.59, 6.00. A bell rang, warning Akosua that she had just one minute to wind up her speech.

"Statistics may well report growth in our Gross Domestic Product," she said, "but those statistics are not reflected in the lives of the poor. The rich build fine new mansions surrounded by high walls topped with razor wire, but the poor continue to live in hovels. Their numbers multiply year by year. Four million of our youth are unemployed or under-employed. Some of them, even at this late hour, are selling dog chains at the traffic lights on Independence Avenue.

"The social effects of poverty, including drug trafficking and other crime, prostitution and child labor, continue to multiply. Poverty leads to environmental degradation, and environmental degradation in turn causes more poverty. A vicious circle; sad, but true."

"I rest my case," Akosua said. "The problem of poverty in Ghana is indeed insoluble. I challenge my brother Osman to demonstrate that it is not."

She glanced up at the screen. The clock showed 6:55. With just five seconds left, she returned to her seat. There was uproarious applause. Her schoolmates rose to their feet, chanting, "A. A! A. A!"

When the applause died down, the MC invited Osman to take his place at the lectern.

Osman cast his eyes over the audience before he spoke. He shook his head.

"That is a hard act to follow," he said at last. "Eloquent, well researched, passionate.

"It is clear that my sister Akosua and I share a hatred of poverty. There can be no doubt that poverty continues to wreck young Ghanaian lives and to humiliate those who survive into adulthood. But we are not debating whether poverty exists in Ghana. We are agreed that it is widespread. What we are debating is whether it can be eliminated or at least drastically reduced. We are debating whether the problem of poverty in Ghana is soluble. My opponent says it is not, basing her argument on the indisputable evidence that one Ghanaian leader after another has failed to solve it. This argument, however, is seriously flawed: failure in the past does not automatically lead to failure in the future. If we are to talk about solutions to the problem of poverty, it is the future we must look to.

"One other thing was lacking in my sister's brilliant presentation: faith; faith in the capacity of Ghanaians, especially young Ghanaians, to learn from the mistakes of their elders in the past and to use those lessons to go on to build a better future.

"One half of our population of 23 million is aged eighteen or less. We have been told that four million young Ghanaians are either unemployed or underemployed. Is our country not a tinder box, subject to sudden ignition by the anger and frustration of our youth?

"It is true that up to now Ghanaian youth have shown little interest in politics as a means of solving their problems. But the world is changing. In Tunisia, in Egypt, in Yemen and Syria, courageous young people have come out onto the streets in recent times, demanding an end to corruption, insisting that their governments must be open and transparent and, in a loud voice, proclaiming their priorities: better access to education and jobs. Jobs before profit.

"Their grassroots activism is a threat to top-down control. Are we young Ghanaians different from young Tunisians or Egyptians? No. It is only a matter of time before we begin to understand our power and to demand a better life. I believe that a new generation of young leaders is about to emerge and that they will be free of the venality of all too many of our elders. Venality, let me remind you, is defined as the use of a position of trust for dishonest gain and openness to bribery and corruption. Our struggle is just beginning."

A young male voice cut the silence: "*A luta continua.*"

"Yeah, yeah," called another.

Osman waited for the uneasy laughter to subside. The MC graciously pressed his 'pause' button.

"So far," Osman continued, "my argument has been based upon speculation and hope. Now I want to offer you a real-life case to demonstrate that, given the right conditions, the problem of poverty in Ghana is indeed soluble."

"The case I propose to examine, " he said and then paused for a few seconds and scanned the audience, almost as if he had forgotten his lines, "That case is me."

He jabbed the middle fingers of both hands into his chest and repeated, "Me."

"My mother grew up in the North, in dire poverty. When she was still young her parents handed her over to a distant relative who brought her to Accra and put her to work as a *kayayo*. After some time she managed to escape from the man's clutches and started trading on her own account, selling onions from a head tray. She was still sleeping rough in Salaga Market when she met my father. He was a police constable.

"I had one junior sister, Afia. All four of us lived in a room, one room, in the police barracks on Nsawam Road. Three years ago my parents both became ill. My father died first and then my mother.

"For my sister Afia the problem of poverty indeed proved to be insoluble. The police commander sent her to the North and put her in the custody of my father's brother, whom she had never seen before. She had to learn to work on his farm, something she had never done in Accra, poor as we were. Then she contracted tuberculosis, a disease of poverty. After we were parted, I saw her again only once, on the afternoon before she died. She was just twelve. A victim of poverty indeed. A young life cut short. A wasted life.

"The story so far would seem to prove Akosua's case. But my story is different. A kind lady, a good Muslim, agreed to adopt me. My second mother, Hajia Zainab, is in the audience tonight. She is a retired school principal. In spite of the fact that she is not rich, she has succeeded in delivering me from poverty. If it were not for her, I might have followed my dear sister to an early grave, or I might be one of those selling dog chains outside.

"Hajia Zainab, Mama as I call her, has set me on a different path, a path paved with books as she says, a path to a life of fulfillment. I doubt if I will ever be rich, but that is because I have no desire to be rich. On the other hand, as a result of her loving care, her attention to my education and, beyond that, her challenge to me to develop my potential and to think for myself, she has given me a life-long insurance policy against poverty. My presence here tonight surely demonstrates that.

"Thank you, Mama."

The auditorium was silent. Osman paused, seemingly to get a grip on his emotions and collect his thoughts. Someone in the audience put two hands together, and then another did the same, and then everyone. In the glare of the stage lights, I saw Akosua pull out a handkerchief to wipe a tear.

The MC stopped the clock during the applause. Now he set it going again. Osman looked up at the screen. He had just 20 seconds left.

"The problem of poverty in Ghana is soluble," he said. "Kwame Nkrumah was right. The key to the solution is education, quality education, education for all. We can do it. All we need is commitment."

It seemed that he had more to say, but his time was up. The bell rang and he returned to his seat.

Of the two supporting speakers, Lily Mends was the more accomplished. Poverty, like death, is not something we joke about in our society; and yet she managed to raise a laugh.

The debaters joined their family members in the front row while the four judges retired to a back room to confer. A young rapper almost stole the show while we waited. His improvised satirical commentary on the debaters and their arguments had the audience convulsed with laughter.

The judges returned and handed two sealed envelopes to the MC, who thanked them.

"Before I let you go," he said, "please tell us what criteria you used in arriving at your decision."

The chief said, "We judged each contribution by its demonstration of analytical skills, by the strength and style of the argument it advanced and by its capacity to hold our attention and interest."

At the MC's invitation, the President joined him on the stage. She wore an elegant *kente kaba* with a head-tie to match.

"Your Excellency," the MC said, "I won't ask you to usurp the role of our judges, but would you care to say something about the overall quality of the debate we've just heard?"

"I'll let you in on a secret," she replied. "I'm seriously considering asking at least one of these young people to join my panel of speech writers."

That drew a laugh and a round of applause.

The MC summoned the debaters back onto the stage and introduced them to the President.

Her Excellency read from the first sealed envelope: "The National Schools Debating Competition. Gold Medal for the Best Team."

Unseen trumpeters blew a fanfare accompanied by a roll of drums. She tore open the envelope and read from the card inside, "The winning team is the Cape Coast Girls High School."

The audience exploded. The girls from Cape Coast danced in the aisles.

Akosua stepped forward. The President shook her hand and said a few words to her. Then she hung a ribbon with a gold medal round her neck and kissed her on both cheeks. Lily was next. Then Osman and Jackson received their silver medals.

The MC handed the second envelope to the President.

She read, "The National Schools Debating Competition. Gold Medal for the Best Speaker."

To the sound of another fanfare, she tore the envelope open and read from the card inside, "The Gold Medal for the Best Speaker goes to Osman Said."

This time it was the boys from Maamobi who clapped and cheered.

Osman received his medal and then Akosua was invited to receive the silver medal for the second best speaker. Osman held out his hand to her. She took it and then gave him a hug. You should have heard the whistles.

Backstage there were long queues waiting to congratulate the winners: family, friends and schoolmates. I saw Osman's Mama, Hajia Zainab, and Akosua's parents, Professor and Mrs. Annan, deep in conversation with Her Excellency the President. The interviews I had planned with Akosua and Osman would have to wait.

Virginia Thompson, Literary, Art and Music Editor, *Ghana Muntie*

CHAPTER 15

Akosua

Akosua Annan. That's me. Aged eighteen years, going on nineteen, and still a virgin. You don't have to believe that but it's true. And not for want of trying, believe me. (Most of the trying, need I say it, has been on the part of the males.)

I reckon I've stopped growing. I've a good body, though a little too broad for the catwalk (except in student shows) and not quite good enough to make it to the national heats of Miss Teen Ghana. Shapely legs that look even better on stilettos and nice firm boobs that can stand up for themselves without a bra for some special occasion. And, so I'm told, a lively expressive face that won me the lead in a recent University Dramatic Society comedy show.

After the National Debating Competition I seriously considered doing Law. The trouble with Law is that you often have to argue a case that you know is wrong. Say, for instance, you have to defend a murderer in court. You know he did it, yet it's your job to destroy the prosecution's case. I decided that that sort of play-acting might be fine for debates but that I didn't want to spend my working life telling lies. I know that murderers are entitled to legal defense. It's just that I don't want to defend them. So I opted for English instead.

After *Inna's Tale* was published in an anthology called

New Writing from Ghana, I had no difficulty getting a place in Legon's creative writing program. I'm now in my second year and I'm already polishing a draft of my first novel. Guess who's helping me? None other than Senior Lecturer Dr. Nana Yaa Mensah, PhD, known in a previous incarnation as Miss Priscilla Mensah. She swears that it was her success in mentoring me for my short story prize that won her the job.

Geraldine Blankson is here, doing Science. She's filled out in all the right places and has become a catwalk champion. We're still good friends. Chastity Baah was here too but got pregnant and dropped out. Lily Mends didn't make it—her SHS results weren't good enough. She's gone to the UK and got admission to a university there. Ama Osei didn't make it either. I think of her often and hope that wherever she is, she's resting in peace.

Well, with all that, especially my novel, you'd think I'd be the happiest girl on the campus. Sadly, that has not been the case. In fact, I've been anything but happy. It seems that I have a relationship problem. For most of my first year things ran pretty smoothly. I was going steady with a Fanti guy called Edgar, a third year law student. I let him kiss me and more and I have to say I enjoyed his company and his caresses. He seemed to have a genuine respect for me, listened to my politics and read my stories. I introduced him to my parents when they came on a visit and they really liked him; at least, that's what they said. I suppose they thought that having a lawyer for a son-in-law might at least be some compensation for not having a lawyer for a daughter.

As the year passed, Edgar became increasingly passionate and demanding. Then a bachelor cousin of his had to travel abroad on business and asked Edgar to look after his apartment. Edgar took me to have a look. Great place: huge plasma screen, fine collection of CDs, old stuff too, that I like so much—Fela, Osibisa, Masekela from down south—a full fridge and freezer and a cupboard full of booze. I cooked him a simple meal, joloff. At the table he insisted on pouring me a full glass of wine. Well, I'm not much of a drinker and I put my hand over the top to block his attempts to give me a refill. In due course he downed the rest of the bottle.

"Edgar," I told him, "go slow. You won't be in a condition to drive me back to campus."

"Who said you're going back to campus?" he asked.

I kept mum but that put me on my guard.

"Let's watch a DVD," he said.

"Fine," I replied. "Do I have a choice?"

I'd browsed through his cousin's collection and been impressed with his taste. Clearly a movie buff.

"No," he said. "Tonight the choice is mine."

What he put on was hard porn from America. Black men and women at a party in a fancy house with a swimming pool, stripping off, all of them and … well you can imagine the rest.

"Edgar," I said, after just a couple of minutes, "I don't want to watch this stuff."

"But I do," he said. "I rented it just for this occasion."

I picked up the remote and switched off the DVD. He had a job controlling his anger.

"Akos," he said, "I have a problem."

"I see that," I said.

"I'm serious," he said. "We need to talk about this."

"Fine," I said. "What's your problem?"

"A build-up of testosterone," he said. "We've been going steady for six months now. It's time to move to the next level."

"You mean you want to …?"

He nodded.

"Edgar," I said. "I'm not ready for that."

I'm not going to tell the whole story here—you'll have to use your imagination to fill in the details. In short, he tried to rape me. I suppose the fact that he was by now quite drunk helped me to escape with no more damage than a ripped blouse. A stream of obscene abuse followed me out of his cousin's front door.

In vino veritas, I guess. Latin: literally, in wine there is truth. The contents of that bottle certainly made Edgar reveal his true nature. The end of the affair. I hailed a cruising taxi.

The next morning I went to share my woes with Aunty Nana Yaa—that's what I call her when no one else is around. We agreed that it would be futile to report the case—it would be Edgar's word against mine. Since then I've steered clear of male students. I've become what, in their arrogance, they call an unguided missile. Until today, that is.

I came out of the English Department after a class and was making my way to the library when I saw *him*. He had his back to me. This guy was bigger than the sixteen-year-old boy I'd known two years before, but I thought at once that it must be him; something about the shape of his shaven head. He was moving away from me. I didn't stop to think.

"Osman!" I called.

It *was* him. He looked round puzzled, clearly wondering who had called his name. Then he saw me. His eyes opened wide, and his mouth too.

"Akosua Annan," he said.

"The very same," I replied.

"*Awaawaawaa,*" he said and held out his hand.

I looked at it and then at his face, his laughing, handsome face.

"*Atuu,*" I said. "Osman, you haven't changed. As shy as ever. A handshake won't do. I want a proper hug. And maybe even a kiss."

Later we sat facing each other across a table in the cafeteria. He kept shaking his head in disbelief.

"I thought I'd lost you," he said. "Not a day has passed that I haven't thought about you."

I put on my stern look.

"Not lewd thoughts, I hope."

"Sometimes," he grinned. "Especially at night. A man is a man is a man."

"Osman," I said. "Will you marry me?"

His eyes again. Those wonderful expressive eyes.

"You can't be serious," he said.

"Of course, I'm serious," I said, but of course, I wasn't.

So there it is. End of story. Seriously. Bye for now.

Glossary and notes

Accra suburbs: Maamobi, Nima, Kaneshie, Roman Ridge

Agoo: salutation announcing the arrival of a visitor ('Is anybody there?) (Reply: amee)

Akan names for girls. There are seven common names, including Afua (Wednesday-born), Ama (Saturday-born) and Akosua or Akos (Sunday-born)

Amu, Ephraim: distinguished Ghanaian composer (1899-1995)

Anansesem: Akan folk-tales, often concerning Ananse, who is both human and a spider

Anomaa: (Twi) bird

Asantehene: king of Ashanti. Those mentioned in the novel are Osei Tutu, Opoku Ware, Osei Kwadwo, Osei Kwame and Prempeh I

Bantama: suburb of Kumasi

BECE: Basic Education Certificate Examination

Book-long: learned, educated

Bron (or Brong): a region of north-west Ghana referred to as Booroom in the title of Sarah Lee's story.

Cape Coast Castle: center of the British slave trade, peaking in the eighteenth century.

Chaley: familiar form of address for male acquaintances.

Cities and towns mentioned in the text: Cape Coast, Saboba, Accra, Anomabu, Koforidua, Kumasi, Wenchi, Tamale, Yendi and Aneho (in Togo) (shown ringed in the map on a following page.)

Ethnic groups and languages: Akan (Fanti, Ashanti, Twi, Nzima), Hausa, Ga, Ewe, Dagomba (language: Dagbani), Konkomba, Frafra, Mossi, Dagaare and Kotokoli.

Ghana Muntie: (Twi) (People of) Ghana, listen! (The name of a newspaper)

Gye Nyame: (Twi) literally: Except God, meaning nothing happens in this world without divine intervention. An Adinkra symbol, often incorporated in the design of mass-produced plastic chairs.

Haj: the Muslim pilgrimage to Mecca.

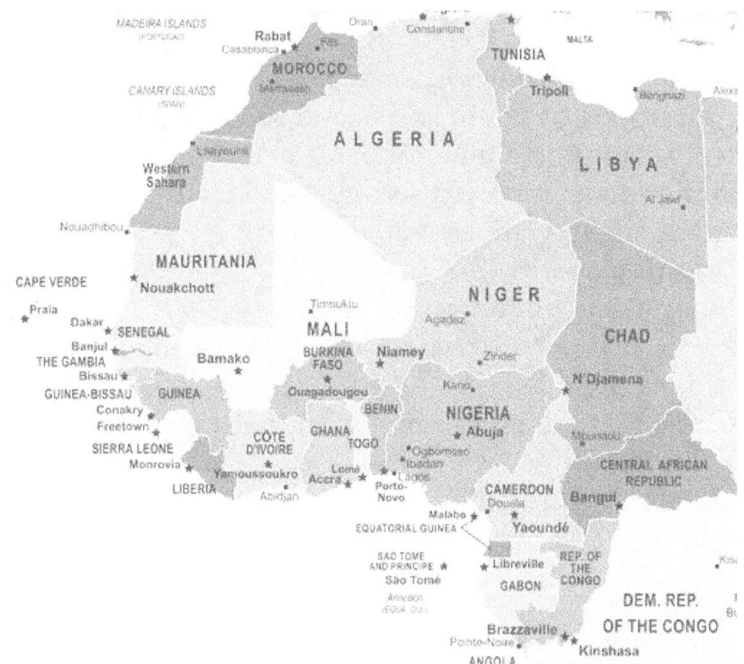

Map of West Africa
Note countries and locations mentioned in the text: Ghana, Madeira (Portuguese), The Gambia (capital: Banjul, formerly Bathurst), Sierra Leone (capital: Freetown)

Harmattan: a dry wind which blows south from the Sahara for a few weeks at the end of the year

Iblis: Arabic for the Devil

JHS: Junior High School

Joloff rice: West African risotto-like dish

Kaba: contraction of "cover shoulder", describing the top half of traditional attire of Ghanaian women.

Kakum forest: tourist site north of Cape Coast.

Kayayo: porter, often a young girl

Kente: traditional Asante woven fabric

Khaki-khaki school: public school

Khaki-khaki: school uniform in public schools

Kotokoraba: suburb of Cape Coast, location of the main market

Krakye: clerk, educated person

Madeira: Portuguese island off the North-west coast of Africa
Madrassa: Islamic religious school
Nkontommere: cocoyam leaves and stew made from them
Obetsebi-Lamptey, Emmanuel: Ghanaian politician (1902-1963)
Oburoni-wawu: imported second-hand clothing
Odwira: Ashanti yam festival
Okro-mouth: gossip
One pound-one pound: inter-city taxi
Osagyefo: savior; title conferred on Dr. Kwame Nkrumah, first
  president of Ghana
Out-dooring: naming ceremony on the seventh day after birth
  of a child
Salaam aleikum: Muslim greeting: peace to you
SHS: Senior High School
Sura: chapter in the Koran
Tro-tro: mini-bus taxi

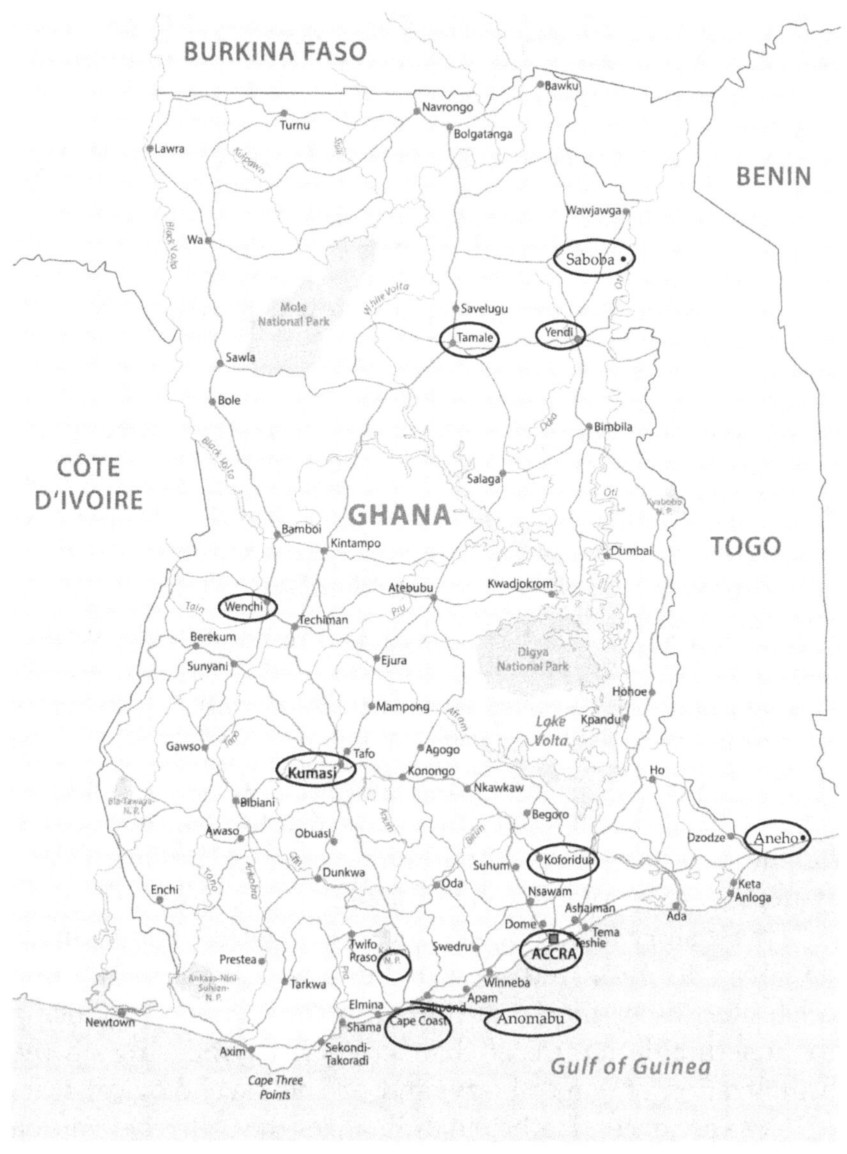

Map of Ghana
Places mentioned in text are ringed

BY THE SAME AUTHOR

Ama: a Story of the Atlantic Slave Trade

Winner of the 2002 Commonwealth Writers Prize for the
Best First Book

"I am a human being; I am a woman; I am a black woman;
I am an African. Once I was free; then I was captured and
became a slave; but inside me, I have never been a slave,
inside me here and here, I am still a free woman."

In the course of four hundred years some twelve million
Africans were forcibly transported across the Atlantic to serve
European settlers and their descendants. Only the barest
fragments of their stories have survived. Manu Herbstein's
ambitious, meticulously researched and moving novel sets
out to recreate one of these lives, following Ama, its eponymous
heroine, from her home in the Sahel, through Kumase at the
height of Asante power, and Elmina, center of the Dutch slave
trade, to a sugar plantation in Brazil.

"This is story telling on a grand scale," writes Tony Simões
da Silva. "In *Ama*, Herbstein creates a work of literature that
celebrates the resilience of human beings while denouncing
the inscrutable nature of their cruelty. By focusing on the
brutalization of Ama's body, and on the psychological scars
of her experiences, Herbstein dramatizes the collective trauma
of slavery through the story of a single African woman. *Ama*
echoes the views of writers, historians and philosophers of
the African diaspora who have argued that the phenomenon
of slavery is inextricable from the deepest foundations of
contemporary western civilization."

The Boy who Spat in Sargrenti's Eye

Winner of the African Literature Association's 2016 award
for the Creative Book of the Year

Sargrenti is the name by which Major General Sir Garnet Wolseley, KCMG (1833 – 1913) is still known in the West African state of Ghana.

Kofi Gyan, the 15-year old boy who spits in Sargrenti's eye, is the nephew of the chief of Elmina, a town on the Atlantic coast of Ghana. On Christmas Day, 1871, Kofi's godfather gives him a diary as a Christmas present and charges him with the task of keeping a personal record of the momentous events through which they are living. This novel is a transcription of Kofi's diary.

Elmina town has a long-standing relationship with the Castelo de São Jorge da Mina, known today as Elmina Castle, built by the Portuguese in 1482 and captured from them by the Dutch in 1637. In April, 1872, the Dutch hand over the unprofitable castle to the British. The people of Elmina have not been consulted and resist the change. On June 13, 1873 British forces punish them by bombarding the town and destroying it. (It has never been rebuilt. The flat open ground where it once stood serves as a constant reminder of the savage power of Imperial Britain.)

After the destruction of Elmina, Kofi moves to his mother's family home in nearby Cape Coast, seat of the British colonial government, where Sargrenti is preparing to march inland and attack the independent Asante state. There Melton Prior, war artist of the London weekly news magazine, *The Illustrated London News*, offers Kofi a job as his assistant. This gives the lad an opportunity to observe at close quarters not only Prior but also the other war correspondents, Henry Morton Stanley and G. A. Henty.

Kofi witnesses and experiences the trauma of a brutal war,

a run-up to the formal colonialism which would be realized ten years later at the 1885 Berlin conference, where European powers drew lines on the map of Africa, dividing the territory up amongst themselves. On February 6, 1874, Sargrenti's troops loot the palace of the Asante king, Kofi Karikari, and then blow up the stone building and set the city of Kumase on fire, razing it to the ground.

Kofi's story culminates in his angry response to the British auction of their loot in Cape Coast Castle. The loot includes the solid gold mask shown on the front cover of the novel. That mask continues to reside in the Wallace Collection in London.

The invasion of Asante met with the enthusiastic approval of the British public, which elevated Wolseley to the status of a national hero. All the war correspondents and several military officers hastened to cash in on public sentiment by publishing books telling the story of their victory. In all of these, without exception, the coastal Fante feature as feckless and cowardly and the Asante as ruthless savages.

The Boy who Spat in Sargrenti's Eye tells the story of these momentous events for the first time from an African point of view. The novel is illustrated with scans of seventy engravings first published in *The Illustrated London News*.

This book won a Burt Award for African Literature which included the donation by the Ghana Book Trust of 3000 copies to school libraries. In 2016, at the annual conference of the African Literature Association held in Atlanta, GA, it received the ALA's Creative Book of the Year Award.

"Manu Herbstein's *The Boy who Spat in Sargrenti's Eye* is a master-work of historical fiction, with the emphasis on historical. The story is set in the events leading up to the creation of the British Gold Coast Colony and Protectorate in 1874, and its main theme is a boy's—and a nation's—struggle to retain dignity in the midst of their loss of independence. Subtly, then, this is an anti-colonial story…the dastardly deeds witnessed by Kofi in this book are very real indeed. Herbstein's magic lies in the way that he reveals them through such a compelling story of a young man caught in the midst of turmoil and change." Prof. Trevor R. Getz, Ph.D. San Francisco State University

Brave Music of a Distant Drum

Sequel to Ama, a Story of the Atlantic Slave Trade

This book is about a slave called Ama. She is old and dying but with an amazing tale to tell; she is blind and cannot write her story, so she tells it to her son. It is a tale of violence, heartache, a story of hope and courage, determination and ultimately love. It is a story of Ghana, of its wonderful people, stolen and taken to a foreign land. Ama - scream your story!!! Glenys Bichan, Cambridge High School Library, New Zealand

There are some stories that touch you and some that change you. This is what Kwame Zumbi discovers after a visit with his blind mother…Award-winning author Manu Herbstein blends fact with fiction to create a rich story that not only tells a heart-wrenching and powerful tale of friendship, love, and loss, but also chronicles the history of the trans-Atlantic Slave Trade and the scars that it has left behind. It's not an understatement to say that Herbstein's tale is a vital part of history and a key to understanding cross-cultural relations today. Keilin Huang, papertigers.org

Manu Herbstein has written an incredible story about the life of Ama, born in Africa but now an aging and blind slave woman in Brazil. She is nearing the end of her life, but is determined she will not go to her grave until her story has not only been told, but written as well. This is a beautifully written, thought-provoking book about age-old questions involving man's inhumanity to man. Betty Kowall, Waterloo Region Record

What a beautiful follow up to "Ama". Talya Honor, Goodreads

Ramseyer's Ghost

2050.

The global village has disintegrated.

The Third World War, ending in a stalemate, has left the planet split between two hostile powers, each with a captive sphere of influence.

The Atlantic Ocean has become an American sea.

Responding to economic decline, the U.S. government has shed ballast, jettisoning areas and populations which make no contribution to the prosperity of its ruling class.

Manifest Destiny is once again the flavor of the day.

West Africa has become a desert of failed states and anarchy, dotted with mines and oil rigs, stockaded and armed by U. S. corporations.

Dumps of toxic waste litter the coast.

From their island outpost of São Tome, the Americans dispatch expeditions of geologists and mining engineers into the dangerous interior of the Dark Continent to search for untapped resources.

One such expedition has gone missing.

Ekem "Crash" Ferguson, born in the U.S. in 2008 of African parents and abandoned to the care of foster parents, is a Captain in the Marine Corps. His career blocked and his marriage failing, he accepts an offer to proceed to Ghana on a one-man mission to find the missing experts.

His arrival in Africa is inauspicious: in a shack amongst the coconut palms he comes across two human skeletons.

This is only the first of his many unexpected discoveries.

President Michelle
or Ten Days that Shook the World

The 2012 U.S. presidential election campaign is well under way when Barack Obama succumbs to a sudden heart attack. Vice-President Biden is sworn in as President and the Democratic Party recalls its convention. Jesse Jackson makes a powerful speech proposing that the party adopt Michelle Obama as its candidate. What happens next?

Some quotes:

"The Act to Restore Democracy to the United States of America...would make it an offense for any candidate for public office to accept gifts or loans in support of his or her election campaign; or, indeed, to use personal wealth for such a purpose. Congress would allocate funds to an Independent Electoral Authority and this Authority would in turn fund the electoral campaigns of all candidates qualified to stand for office...At a stroke, this law would level the electoral playing field. For the first time in generations the wealthy would have little or no advantage over the poor in the competition for office. She expected new talents to emerge which would enrich and invigorate American political life. New parties might enter the political arena, breaking the monopoly presently shared by Republicans and Democrats and breathing new life into American democracy...."

"In the first year of my Presidency I shall close down, that is, disarm and evacuate, all our military bases abroad; and hand them over either to the host country, or, if the hosts agree, to the United Nations. All our warships will return to their home ports, tasked with patrolling our own shores, not those of other nations."

She characterized the Middle East, Israel and occupied Palestine, as a "festering wound that has infected the body politic of much of our world." "The so-called two-state solution," she said, was clearly no solution to anything and would no longer receive American support. "In its stead," she said, "I propose to use all the means at my disposal to persuade the parties to negotiate, in a broadly representative national convention, the constitution of a single secular state within the pre-1948 boundaries of Palestine, a constitution that will guarantee full protection for both individual human rights and for the rights of all religious communities."

"What I am tentatively staking out here today," she said, "is a case for leadership, for American leadership. But leadership of a different kind, leadership based not on economic and military power. No. Not that. Not that. I ask, with all humility, that my leadership be judged and that this country's leadership be judged, from this day on, on moral grounds."

www.ingramcontent.com/pod-product-compliance
Lightning Source LLC
Chambersburg PA
CBHW071434300726

48976CB00004B/1323